HOUSE of CARDS

Nat Burns

Bella
BOOKS
2010

Bella Books, Inc.
P.O. Box 10543
Tallahassee, FL 32302

Printed in the United States of America on acid-free paper
First Edition 2010

Editor: Katherine V. Forrest
Cover Designer: Linda Callaghan

ISBN 13: 978-1-59493-203-8

Also by Nat Burns

Two Weeks in August

To the many interesting people in the small towns where I've lived. You've inspired this book.

Acknowledgments

Thank you Bella Books, for bringing readers my way. And for giving me Katherine V. Forrest as an editor. She's amazing.

About the Author

Nat Burns has worked as a waitress, greenhouse laborer, cashier, book/movie/music reviewer, staff reporter, freelance journalist, teacher, media coordinator, journal compositor, managing editor, computer support technician and an editorial systems coordinator. Through it all there has remained one constant: she's always been a novelist.

CHAPTER ONE

Spring 1985

Another marathon gin rummy game was underway at Ellie Grayson's house just off Catholic Boulevard in the town of Freshwater, North Carolina. Unlike many card games, with smoke-filled dimness framing wary poker faces, this gathering was comprised of Craig County's finest matrons, prim and heavy from years of unwavering moral judgments.

On a nearby sideboard, on lace and silver, reclined sweet and salty tidbits, prepared earlier in the day by Ellie's "girl," Salutey Taliaferro. More compelling, however, was the rack of bottles standing ready for service behind the laden platters. Ellie's fully stocked bar was a source of great pride.

"Did any of you see *The Oprah Winfrey Show* Friday?" asked

Beverly Powell, loose skin under her chin trembling with each word. She asked the question of the room in general and her eyes remained on the fan of cards she held.

"What was it about?" queried Ellie as her dimpled hand discarded the king of spades.

"Exotic dancers," Beverly returned. "Imagine the nerve of those women gettin' up there and strutting naked as the day they were born. I've never seen the like."

"Now, *that* I believe," muttered Kaylen Stauder as she nudged Jane Anne Viar with an elbow just bony enough to be painful. Jane Anne snickered, trying to conceal the merriment with one hand across her mouth. Her cards, fanned neatly in her other hand, slid from her fingers and she swooped forward to catch them.

"I don't know," Ellie said, as she thoughtfully poked one thumb inward toward her plush, overweight body. "If I still had my figure, I might do it."

"What figure? You never had a figure," Margaret Trimball said in a teasing way. She winked a bleary eye, clearly intoxicated. She allowed her tongue to loll from her mouth in a comic expression.

"I can see Ellie up there now," announced Jeanie Saunders. "Shakin' that thing."

"Well," Ellie muttered in her own defense. "They do have some big-boned gals who do that type of dancing."

Kaylen belted out the first lines of Carole King's song "I Feel the Earth Move" as she gathered up the entire discard pile.

"Why is it the skinny ones always pick," Ellie whined.

"I enjoyed the one about the men who dress up as women," interjected Jeanie, scrutinizing her hand.

"The one about transvestites," offered Margaret. "I saw that show."

"Transvestites?" repeated Ellie. "What's that?"

"Like she said," answered Margaret slowly. "Men who like to dress up in women's clothes."

"Oh, right," scoffed Beverly. "Who'd want to do that?"

Margaret giggled, drawing all eyes her way. She waved the attention away and took another deep pull of her vodka tonic. But she squirmed, clearly wanting to say something. Faced with so many waiting faces, she succumbed.

"It's not an illness, you know," she informed the room a trifle too loudly. "It's perfectly normal, really. Men have always done it. Women, too."

Crickets sang love sonnets outside the open windows of Ellie's antique-filled dining room, pale blue drapes slapped time with each gust of breeze. The musty scent of Ellie's dusting powder hung heavy in the air and Kaylen began to sense trouble. It was a simple thing really, the portents; the subtle twitch of a lip, the raised brow, the indolent sniff.

Don't say anything else, Margaret, Kaylen willed.

"It's called cross-dressing," Margaret continued, "and the number of people doing it is on the rise, or so I hear."

"Cross-dressing." This terse comment came from Beverly, who wore an expression of genteel repugnance.

The card game was forgotten as most of the women craned forward with slow eagerness. Jane Anne fiddled nervously with her fan of cards, the sound a loud staccato drumbeat in the silence of the room.

Margaret, who never remembered to stop at her third vodka, leaned forward, the smell of her newly-permed hair wafting to Kaylen.

"Can you keep a secret?" she asked, one forefinger crooking unnecessarily in front of her mouth.

Kaylen's head began a slow monotone movement back and forth. *Margaret, no.* She wanted very badly to interject a new topic but her tongue felt thick and wanted to cling to the roof of her mouth. Then it was too late; worlds of damage had been done.

"Ernie and I do it," Margaret admitted with a triumphant toss of her head. "Right down to our underwear."

Silence swelled as all tried to picture rough Ernie Trimball, who operated his own car repair business on Third Street, in lace panties and satin slips. Almost as difficult was imagining

Margaret attired in jockey shorts and men's shoes.

A titter of laughter grew as the mental images found a foothold.

"It's all right," Margaret assured the women, her palms struggling to push down air in an effort to squelch the rising hilarity. Her face reddened and her dark eyes rolled wildly as she realized the trauma of her careless words.

"Ernie? Your Ernie? And you?" Ellie screeched.

"Once, we only did it once. Besides, I think it does people good to experience..." Her voice trailed off, lost amid a barrage of laughter and chortled comment.

Jane Anne turned to Kaylen, her dusky blue eyes troubled. Kaylen returned the glance, her own gaze conveying helplessness.

"Well, it's getting late," said Beverly, trying to inject a serious manner. Her thin fingers skittered across the table, gathering cards, as she choked back laughter.

Kaylen studied her, seeing a covered saucepan on the verge of boiling over. She can't wait to tell someone else, she realized with a lurch of distaste. She rose and carried her empty glass into the kitchen. Placing the glass in the sink, she leaned forward, feeling sick.

Supporting her weight with her palms and the twin pillars of her arms, she lowered her shoulders and stared into the dark void of the drain. Inside, as clearly as any soothsayer, she saw the future.

Within days everyone in town would know about the Trimballs. It was something new to gossip about. Best of all it gave the people of the town, especially those who may have fantasized about cross-dressing, a target and a scapegoat. Huge lace undies would be left in cars turned in for repair at Trimball's garage; a worthwhile joke even though it would lead to an inordinate number of mechanical breakdowns. Eventually Ernie and Margaret would leave town, find a new home.

After a lifetime of living in Freshwater, Kaylen knew what to expect. She'd seen it when Markie Ellis had fallen in love with the married preacher. And when the Christie sisters had been arrested for working as prostitutes in a town forty miles north.

It didn't take much for arbitrary ostracism. It could be something as simple as allowing your goats to get into a neighbor's cornfield once too often. Kaylen sighed and peered out into the spring darkness on the other side of the kitchen window. The view reminded her of Freshwater. A black hole where people sometimes just disappeared, one way or another.

CHAPTER TWO

Spring sunlight leapt across the craggy peaks of Old Pine Ridge and raced with frantic haste through the green sloping fields of central North Carolina. The sunlight slowed and crept warily into the slumbering town of Freshwater, brightening streets and tall sides of ancient wood-frame buildings with a gentle hand.

Kaylen, sitting in her home just outside town, calmly watched its approach.

The sunbeam painted the worn floorboards of her living room, then invaded upward slowly, highlighting the left arm of the ragged easy chair in which she sat, splashing welcome heat across her bare thighs. Its measured tread slowed and stopped when the brightness reached the gold-framed, pastel-tinted picture of Jesus resting on a small table next to her. The light made Jesus's halo glow even brighter and his eyes suddenly lit with something stronger than compassion.

"Oooh, Jesus wants me," Kaylen announced to the empty room, her voice filled with awe. She experienced an inordinate thrill of satisfaction at speaking the sacrilege aloud. The smell of fresh-brewed coffee beckoned irresistibly so she didn't linger to apologize to Jesus. Expressing a grunt of effort, she lifted her skinny, arthritis-badgered body and padded barefoot into the kitchen to fetch a cup.

The sunlight had settled in and its warmth, felt through the many large, cheerful windows of the spacious kitchen, sat heavy on Kaylen's shoulders as she poured a mug of the dark brew. After stewing in thought for several moments, Kaylen decided it was Monday. Yes, church yesterday, today was definitely Monday and that meant brunch with Jane Anne.

Kaylen crossed to the white, naked refrigerator and reluctantly peered inside. There wasn't much there and she accepted the fact that a trip to Lerner's Grocery couldn't be avoided much longer. But there was milk, and eggs, and fruit only slightly shriveled, coffee and juice. These offerings would satisfy Jane Anne.

A long look through the screen of the back door informed her that the slanting sun had already begun to steam the dew from her small garden. Leaf lettuce shimmered pale green in the new daylight, bordered on either side by the darker greens of beans and peppers. Her peas provided one more interesting shade of green, especially when laid against the verdancy of the surrounding mountains off in the distance. It was going to turn into another hot spring day.

Kaylen returned to her bedroom. As the only windows faced west, sunlight had not yet brightened this room and Kaylen sank gratefully onto the bed, her coffee mug barely making the safety of the nightstand. Thoughts gamboled through her head and she closed her eyes to better experience the images created by her fertile imagination.

She was soaring high above the fields of fescue and rye that stretched as far as the eye could see, just outside the environs of Freshwater. Her pink cape fluttered about her shoulders and her body was sleek and strong in its crimson leotard.

She waved to Fred Pritchard, out feeding his Charolais cows in the fenced field just north of his big frame farmhouse. Hearing the wind of her passage, he looked for her and returned her wave cheerfully as she passed overhead.

Farther on, a whole family of hired workers labored in Osh Payen's cotton field, picking the dregs left after the monstrous machinery had gone through. With their white-kerchiefed heads, the women looked like so many cotton balls themselves.

She saw an unusual traffic jam farther along the main highway that connected Freshwater to other cities and towns west. A truck carrying steers to Jim Henway's cattle auction had turned over... No. Wait. The back gate had come loose and one of the cows had tumbled into the road. Several men, commuters who had parked their cars and joined in, worked to round up the frightened, bawling cow. Kaylen flew in to help and the job was accomplished in the blink of an eye.

Polly Withers was hanging out clothes, just as she did every morning Kaylen passed by. The woman had to get up at dawn to begin washing for her huge brood. Mounds of wet clothing were stacked in tattered baskets next to the clotheslines but with Kaylen's help they were stretched taut across the lines within minutes.

After making her rounds across the area, Kaylen flew to the deserted barn where the lover always waited for her. The lover didn't have a name, but certainly had a form, one that lingered in her mind long after their time together was through.

The figure coming to her was small and spare of form; but rounded, with plump muscles. She loved to run her fingers through the long, soft hair. Her imaginary lover wore one thing only, a pair of cut-off denim overalls, and waited anxiously for her, skin hot and familiar. The face was usually shadowed but she was certain great compassion and love shone from the clear blue eyes. Hesitant hands were soft as small hamsters yet roamed her body freely.

The images faded abruptly and Kaylen's hands left her small, yielding breasts to reach listlessly toward her coffee. She was simply too lazy and disconnected today to enjoy the fantasy life and love she had created years ago. Embarrassed and confused by what felt like loss, she rose, stripped off her sleepshirt and went into the bathroom to shower.

CHAPTER THREE

"I really think she meant something like Kay Lynn or Katie Lynn," said Jane Anne later that morning. She was working on ingesting a pile of fruit-smothered waffles so her remarks were interspersed with dead air as she chewed. "And I don't care what your daddy says. I don't think she would have named you Karen."

It was an old argument and fair bored Kaylen to tears.

"It really doesn't matter, Jane Anne. I'm Kaylen and Kaylen is what I'll stay," she sighed, picking desultorily at her own waffles. The shrunken, pockmarked wafers seemed to eye her with evil intent. With fork as weapon, she began dissecting the monsters into nanoparticles.

Kaylen's mother had died after giving birth to her only baby girl, managing to fill in the name on the birth certificate as

10

blood flowed from her body in a killing tide. The middle name, Bluefield, was understandable enough, being the name of her mother's prominent southern family but the name Kaylen had everybody scratching their head. There was just no handle on it at all. An unfamiliar or unusual name was all right as long as there was a television character or actor with the name, or perhaps, if the name was that of a favored heroine from literature. After all, there was a Gloria Swanson Campbell just down the road, a Scarlet Goad in Freshwater Tavern, and a DeMille Godfrey who lived just across the South Carolina line. There were even Marilyn Monroes by the handful and it was accepted. But a Kaylen?

All that naming insanity had happened forty years ago this past February and Kaylen had heard enough speculation about her name to last three lifetimes. And Jane Anne was still at it.

"Hey, Jane Anne," Kaylen interrupted easily, "have you got your peas in the ground yet?"

Caught off guard, but in true southern lady tradition, Jane Anne recovered quickly.

"Why no, Kaylen, I told you that last week, remember? I swear, you must be getting senile. Are you all right?"

Jane Anne peered closely at her friend. "You do look a little flushed," she added, a worried note to her voice.

"For goodness' sake, Jane Anne, I'm just trying to tell you that you'd better get those peas in the ground soon or it'll be too late. You gotta pay attention to the seasons if you plan on having a garden."

Jane Anne straightened her back, moving her tall, lanky frame into a prim and proper board. "Well, thank you, ma'am."

Kaylen watched her friend with dour brown eyes finally smiling wide enough to show the gold tooth installed at great expense two years ago by Dr. Prince, local dentist and part-time party magician.

Jane Anne returned the smile and took another bite of waffle. "Besides," she continued after chewing and swallowing, "why should I plant peas when I can get all I want from you?"

She smiled victoriously and just barely avoided Kaylen's

amiable slap to her forearm. They fell into a comfortable silence, eating, sipping juice, clearing throats now and again.

Looking out the window of the dining room which faced north, Kaylen watched as clouds passing overhead patterned dark shadows on her side yard.

"Do you ever think about sex anymore, Jane Anne?" Kaylen asked in a musing tone. "I sure have been thinking about it a lot lately."

Jane Anne reacted as if she'd been struck. Quickly, with delicate precision, she placed her fork by her plate and lifted a napkin to her lips.

"Now, Kaylen," she began nervously, "I've told you I don't like to talk about such things. It isn't proper."

"Oh, what is proper?" Kaylen said loudly, rising from the table and fetching her first cigarette of the day from a pack lying on the kitchen counter. Her left hand hooked an ashtray and she returned to the table.

Jane Anne eyed her restless friend with a disapproving stare. "I don't know what gets into you sometimes, Kaylen. You're just like a wild stallion that hasn't been broken. You've always got some kind of fanciful notion."

Kaylen took a deep drag from her cigarette and blew the smoke in Jane Anne's frowning face. Then she smoothed her cropped, graying hair, cut just three weeks ago because all her friends said she was getting too old to have long hair straggling down her back.

"God, I miss my hair."

"You miss your hair? What has that got to do with..." Jane Anne lifted her hands in a gesture of futility. "I give up. Your mind has no rhyme or reason. I think all those drugs in college really messed up your brain."

Kaylen smiled. College. Constant parties, grass, acid, pills and booze. She had moved through her college years in a Technicolor fog and as she got older, she realized those were probably the best years of her life. She was one of the many people who remembered college with fondness. At least it gave her something to care about. Kaylen worried that her immature college days would never really leave her. She still wore tie-dyed T-shirts when she could get away with it, and also the Earth Shoes, although today they were called Birkenstocks and sold for upward of one hundred dollars a pair at the stores in Raleigh.

She had enjoyed the freedom of her college years. People had been so comfortable then. The only problem was those who were the most comfortable were the ones you lost touch with first. They were off right away being so very comfortable with the next person in line.

"I think maybe I'd better go now," Jane Anne stated with uncommon firmness as she watched her friend's face. "I don't think you're in the mood for company today."

Kaylen smiled ruefully and smashed her cigarette in the ashtray.

"I'm sorry, Jane Anne. Really. I'll quit being such a poop. How about a game of rummy?"

Jane Anne cut her eyes sideways at Kaylen, as if judging whether to trust the woman.

"No more talk of...you know...sex?" she coaxed in a warning tone.

Kaylen nodded immediately and fetched the deck of cards from a carved wooden box under one of the big kitchen windows.

"I would give a lot for a really good orgasm though," she said, smirking as she resumed her seat. "How about you?"

Jane Anne looked suddenly as if she'd swallowed a very big, very nasty insect.

CHAPTER FOUR

Jane Anne parked her small truck carefully in the drive of her rental cottage and let out a loud whoosh of breath. Lately, time with Kaylen left her feeling strange somehow, maybe inadequate, certainly confused.

And what was this new thing, this sex business? Why did Kaylen have to bring up the one subject Jane Anne avoided?

It was an opportunity, her rational mind whispered, *an opportunity to tell her how you feel.*

But how did she feel, really? Could she tell Kaylen she had feelings that terrified her, feelings she could never hope to deal with alone? Would Kaylen understand if Jane Anne spilled out the haunting erotic images that chased her night after night? Or would they chase Kaylen away just as mercilessly as they chased her?

Kaylen was Jane Anne's best friend, their friendship launched with a shared smile and eye contact during a gathering of the local civic group called the Freshwater Magnolias. The smile had erupted when big-mouthed, know-it-all Jeanie Saunders referred to that Florida writer, that "Franklin" Hemingway, who had written all those violent, disturbing books in the "Twenties and Thirties."

Jane Anne had been new in town then, and though Kaylen had stepped right in earlier to make her feel she'd been there forever, it was that sparkling, tolerant smile, that thank-God-there's-you-and-me grin that had clinched the friendship so many years ago. Memories of those long ago smiles gave birth to a new one as Jane Anne left her truck and walked into her home.

Filtered daylight mantled her furniture with a possessive hand and the smile faded as Jane Anne realized this daylight was the only living thing there to welcome her. She pushed depression aside and with forced cheer slammed her handbag onto the hall table.

"I'm home!" she announced to the empty living room, deciding for the umpteenth time that she really needed to get a cat, or at the very least, a bird. She could have stayed on in Georgia, near her family, if she had wanted to, but it was real hard living single—a spinster—in the town where one had grown to adulthood.

You were such a lovely girl, the Georgia townsfolk would point out when they cornered her, *it's a shame no man ever appealed*. Then they'd start listing names and pedigrees with a hopeful mien, waiting for one to spark an interest. But the interest never came and the people would eventually leave her alone, only to return later with a new list. This cycle repeated endlessly and when Jane Anne found herself blissfully counting the proliferating gray hairs of these well-intentioned busybodies as they prattled on, she had known it was time to get out. Freshwater, North Carolina seemed as good a place as any.

A library science major in college, Jane Anne was more than qualified for the position of Freshwater librarian. The ad, in a well-known library periodical, had been a simple one but it seemed gilt-edged and forty feet high when Jane Anne had spotted it.

The first weeks in Freshwater had been easy ones; she was actually happy for the reprieve into solitude. Eventually it grew wearying, though, and Jane Anne allowed a gradual blooming outward from herself, seeking some type of companionship. It was about this time Kaylen came into the library, a two-foot stack of books crippling her arms. Each book had been hopelessly overdue but Kaylen paid the fines cheerfully, her eyes already scanning the new release rack for fresh fodder.

Kaylen was a slow and methodical chooser of reading material; she was in the library for more than three hours, the entire time involved in book selection. Jane Anne watched her warily, wondering at this lanky, middle-aged woman with long unbrushed tendrils of gray hair. The one time she had taken her oblique gaze away, to load the final books onto a shelving cart, Kaylen was suddenly behind her.

"You're new here. What's your name?"

Jane Anne, caught off guard by the sneak attack, could only focus on Kaylen's unique scent—tobacco smoke laced with spicy Jontue perfume—and not on her words.

"You okay?" Kaylen asked finally, brown eyes turning worried as they studied her. "I didn't mean to scare you."

Jane Anne mentally chided herself. Some way to make a good impression in a new town! She quickly scrambled for composure.

"You didn't scare me really...just...Jane Anne. My name is Jane Anne Viar," she managed to say.

"Well, welcome, Jane Anne, and let me say I hope you enjoy our little town. There's not much to do here but we do it earnestly."

Silence fell as Kaylen studied her. Jane Anne began chafing under the steady regard.

"Kaylen, by the way, Kaylen Stauder. I live out south of town, on Twenty-Four."

Knowing a similar response was expected, Jane Anne replied in kind. "I live over on the North Acres property."

"The Jackson house?" Kaylen was suitably surprised.

"Oh, no, just the gatekeeper's cottage." Jane Anne laughed at the ridiculous idea of living in the Jackson mansion, now owned by wealthy Randolph Wallace. "On my salary, I couldn't even wash the windows of that place."

Kaylen laughed. "You and me both, sweetie."

Another long, thoughtful pause. Kaylen spoke again.

"Listen, I'm looking for this book, I can't remember the name of it but it's a journal kept by this elderly Amish gal..."

And that was the beginning. Jane Anne spent a hilarious twenty minutes hunting down the title and location of that particular book and by the end of that time had agreed to attend the second official meeting of the Freshwater Magnolias. The five years since had been a slow, smooth coast. Her life was actually very pleasant. She had a good job, with little real stress, a good friend whom she could spend time with, and whatever time was left over was spent reading her beloved books, doing a little gardening, and working on the novel she was trying to write.

Jane Anne kicked off her shoes and dropped into the desk chair. Staring at her own face in the dark, shuttered face of her computer, she thought of her mother. And about how her mother would hate the simple, dull life Jane Anne lived.

Tansy Parkes Viar was still a beautiful woman, even though she had recently celebrated her sixty-eighth birthday. The cream of Atlanta society, she had married into the *nouveau riche* Viar family, a move she regretted even before the honeymoon had gotten into full swing. Not that Malcolm Viar wasn't a handsome man, he was that and more, but he had the mental energy of a dead goldfish and certain mannerisms, including an appalling boorishness, annoying over time, lent proof to his lack of good breeding. To make up for this obvious faux pas in judgment, Tansy set out on a path of fanatical social networking, trying to make sure her family measured up to Atlanta's elite; the world she had been born into.

This mission, of course, made her into a harridan as far as her henpecked new husband was concerned, and later her son and daughter.

Jane Anne's older brother, Martin, had been so affected by his mother's constant, domineering control that, upon reaching early adulthood, he had disappeared into the jungles of Belize. Now, thirty years later, no one was sure of his whereabouts.

Jane Anne, ever the dutiful daughter, had stayed home. Had matriculated at all the right schools, had participated in a proper "coming out" with its attendant parties and parade of eligible bachelors. Her seeming ineptness for seeking a marriage partner had angered her mother.

Perhaps it was this ability to stir a reaction that caused Jane Anne obstinately to refuse to accept any of the proposals that were proffered. Then it became too late; the proposals trickled as suitors took up new and more likely conquests. And Jane Anne became a librarian.

She had no regrets. She knew she was certainly happier alone than she would have been with any of her erstwhile suitors. Still, she felt alienated from her world. It seemed as if she never really fit in anywhere unless she wore the uniform of genteel politeness so required in southern society. And so that daily cloak was donned though a huge part of Jane Anne wanted to stand naked atop the Baptist church and yell out all that she believed she could be—a person far removed from what those in her life assumed her to be.

She stuck out her tongue at her mottled reflection and switched on the computer. Dim green light snatched at her face and took it away leaving a menu of commands that would give access to the manuscript she was working on. For some reason her hand paused, perched delicately above the keyboard like the neck of a snoozing swan.

Was it in her now to write? To precisely portray the passions and tempests that moved her characters along their imagined journey? Didn't writers compose their best work during times of intense trouble and conflict?

She sighed, clicked off the machine and pushed away from the desk. What real trouble did she have? Only the thoughts that hammered at her day and night, thoughts of freedom and release, thoughts of escape from the proper boredom of her life.

Her hand crept to the end table next to the sofa, picked at a library book. Jane Anne lifted the book and opened it. Moments later she was far from Freshwater, North Carolina, living in another town and in another skin, becoming part of the tragedy and joy of other lives. A place immeasurably better than dealing with the unfulfilled reality of her own life.

CHAPTER FIVE

Eda Byrne slammed her foot onto the brake pedal of the company truck and slid the truck with fearless abandon into the cleared area directly in front of the door to Helios Landscaping. Leaping from the driver's seat with her usual jack-in-the-box impetuosity, Eda narrowly missed plowing her tiny form into a young man and woman who were exiting the business. Despite her profuse apologies, the couple watched her with angry disbelief as they seated themselves into their spanking-clean Taurus sedan. Eda laughed helplessly, turning her head so they wouldn't see. She stepped into the landscaping office.

More a full-fledged greenhouse, the "office" extended a good seven hundred feet past the front entrance. Large panes of Plexiglas had been framed together, with obvious skill and great expense, to form a domed roof that sank almost to the ground on either side of the wide building. Tables, in an infinite variety of shapes and styles, stretched all the way to the end. Eda often wondered how these tables, some older than she, managed to support the many flats and pots of dirt and greenery they were called upon to bear.

A deep intake of breath brought Eda the familiar and exhilarating smells of new growing plants as well as the dark and rich birth-smell of fresh dirt.

"Whatcha know, kiddo?" called Suzanne from her seat at a secondhand school teacher's desk set against the far right wall.

Eda waved to the large goddess of a woman, who easily weighed several hundred pounds, with a wide placid countenance and lazy green eyes. Her long brown hair, graying rapidly, was normally worn in a braid that rambled along her back. Today her hair was loose and the thick glory of it mantled her wide shoulders and heavy arms.

"Hey, babycakes," Eda added in greeting as she crossed to fetch a cola from the company refrigerator.

Suzanne grunted absently, her attention suddenly captured by an order she held in her hand.

Eda studied her employer, wondering if she was troubled. Suzanne was often troubled. Her husband Carl was a hard drinker and a womanizer. Add three teenaged children into the stew and Suzanne usually had her hands full.

"Everything okay?" Eda asked, pausing to breathe after downing half the soda.

"Huh?" Suzanne's head lifted. "Oh, just trying to make sense out of what the Shermans say they want."

"Those two that were just in here?"

"Ummhmm. And please, would you stop rushing around like your pants are on fire? The Shermans think we're weird enough as it is without you knocking them flat."

Eda blushed at being caught in the act, but her attention was piqued. "Weird? Weird, how?"

"You know, the usual." Suzanne reared back in her chair to give Eda her full attention. "A business run entirely by women,

women shirking their wifely duties by working outside the home."

Eda replied with a knowing nod of her head. "And that's the very reason why most of them are divorced or separated, because they refuse to take their jobs as wives and mothers seriously."

Suzanne smiled, but sourly. "It's hard to believe a nice up-and-coming couple like the Shermans thinks that way."

"Yeah," Eda agreed hollowly. "If only they knew."

"It wouldn't really make a difference. So what if all our employees are past victims of domestic violence? So what Pattie had her left eyeball gouged out by her ex-husband's thumb? By way of the thinking of most people in this town, we're only promoting that sort of violence because we're encouraging women to 'get above' themselves and forget who they really are."

Silence fell as Eda sipped her drink. Suzanne laced her fingers together atop her ample belly and gazed out the window. Traffic billowed by on the two lanes of Route 420 that led to Fayetteville and on to Interstate 95 that could take you south of anywhere.

Eda plopped into the swivel chair opposite her boss and spun all the way around, splaying out her small body. "Damn, the people in this town are annoying!"

"Shhh!" Suzanne cautioned comically. "You're going to get us all tarred and feathered with your radical talk."

Eda's strange tinkling laugh burst forth and the already brilliant room seemed to brighten momentarily. "I don't care, Suzy, and you know it."

Suzanne smiled fondly upon this youngest, but sharpest, member of her crew. "How's Cora's cat?"

"Good, for now." Eda used the index fingernail on one hand to pick idly at the calluses on the palm of the other. "There's nothing much anybody can do. When a cat's that old and in that much pain, the kindest thing, by far, is to—"

"But Cora won't do it, will she?" Suzanne's thoughtful gaze roamed Eda's face.

Eda was a natural born veterinarian and was often called

upon to help out with the local pets. Everyone in town talked about the way the animals felt at ease with Eda, almost talked to her, for goodness sake.

But Cora Aimes' much loved cat, Hitler, a belligerent ball of ragged fur, half blind and stricken by a knobby type of arthritis, treated Eda and her ministrations with amused tolerance at best.

Eda shrugged. "We'll probably bury the two of them together."

Suzanne snorted and shuffled the papers on her desk. "Listen, the Shermans want a water garden so I'm giving it to Cary. I want you to do the Stauder job. Did you ride by there this morning?"

The bell over the door sounded and both women looked up simultaneously. Oddly enough, a hard gust of wind had moved the door because there was no one there. As they watched, however, a thin brown hand snaked around the corner and pressed against the metal door handle. A woman appeared. She was small, dark-haired, with one of the sweetest, most angelic faces ever imagined by a creator. She stepped inside and her dark eyes caressed Eda briefly.

"Hey, Becca," Suzanne called. "I thought it was your day off."

"Was," Becca replied, her voice carrying a hint of Hispanic music. "I just came to get the clippers. Tomas wants to cut those big hedges today."

Suzanne's gaze slid sideways toward Eda who had shrunken into her chair and paled perceptibly.

"Don't you let him work out in this sun too long. Days like this are killers, I don't care what month it is, it's still hot."

"I won't, sure." Becca lifted the electric clippers from a pile of machinery near the south wall and walked slowly toward the front door. The slim fingers of her free hand fiddled nervously with the tail of the light cotton shirt she wore above worn jeans. Her eyes rested on Eda again. Pausing at the thick glass door, she glanced at Suzanne and smiled tremulously.

"Well, I'll go then. Thank you." One more quick glance at

Eda and she was gone.

"Kiss that baby for me," Suzanne called after her. Becca waved through the glass to show she heard.

"Umm, I sure did. It's pretty big, if she wants the whole thing. Did she say?" Eda carried on the conversation as if there had been no interruption but began anxiously gnawing one thumbnail.

A long silence stretched until Suzanne cleared her throat. Her eyes were gentle as she leaned forward. "You okay, honey?"

Eda looked up abruptly, her attitude combative. "Why wouldn't I be?"

"Yeah," Suzanne frowned and sat back. "Well, obviously, seeing Becca again."

"It's all right, Suze. I know what you do, scheduling us so we don't have to work together and all. I appreciate that, I really do. She's made her choice though, and that's that. We'll get along."

"Tomas is a good man, honey. I'm sure it was a hard choice for her."

Eda's laugh was scornful. "Got pregnant pretty quick, didn't she. Seems like it was easy enough."

"Now, Eda..." Suzanne began but the younger woman cut her off with a dismissive gesture.

"It's okay, Suze. Really." Her gaze was calm and steady as she snared the older woman's attention. "Now, did the Stauder woman say what she wanted?"

Suzanne sighed heavily. "No, she didn't say how much of the yard she wanted done. You'll have to go out and check on that later this week, as soon as you can. That resort job put us behind."

"Stauder's up to speed. I've already got it laid out."

Suzanne rose and moved slowly back into the greenhouse, one hand absently tugging at the wide seat of her faded jeans. "I don't see how you can do that, just look at a place and know what's right. I'd be half crazy if I was as good as you are. Well, come on back here and tell me what you think you'll need so I can make sure I've got it all set aside for you."

Suzanne's voice faded as Eda's mind whirled. She was once

again in Becca's arms, the sweet-spicy scent of Becca enfolding and intoxicating her. She was once more falling into the warm, fuzzy depths of Becca's dark eyes.

Angrily, Eda pushed these images away and focused instead on the details of the Stauder yard. Hard as she tried, however, she kept seeing Becca in front of her, Becca standing in the sunlit doorway saying goodbye, saying she had chosen to be Tomas's wife instead of Eda's dearest love and partner.

"Ahhh, hell," Eda whispered and pressed her eyes closed with trembling fingers. The Stauder yard, the Stauder yard.

Whether blessed or cursed with it, she had a photographic memory. Eda's life was a perpetual rehashing of remembered events and ideas.

Nothing was forgotten, no event seemed new to her and so she was often bored. Working with nature was the one thing that helped keep her sane; it changed so often and so quickly from day to day that even Eda, with her cataloguing memory couldn't keep up.

She really should have gone to college, if for no other reason than stimulating her mind to new heights. Eda had balked, able only to visualize more of the same monotony as in high school —amazed instructors, alienation from her peers and quick, complete mastery of all the material put in front of her. Where was the challenge in that?

And then there had been Becca. For three years there had been Becca. Then she was gone and Eda was still here.

She had planned on going to school to become a veterinarian, a career she was sure she would have loved. After meeting and falling for Becca, they began working at Helios together. Suzanne, who had just started the landscaping business with a small group of friends, knew Eda's mother from time spent volunteering together at the woman's shelter east of Freshwater and she had welcomed Eda aboard.

Getting in on the ground floor and being able to make many of the formative decisions for the business had given Eda a sense of self-confidence and satisfaction. With help from a horticulture course at the community college, she became a certified landscape engineer within a matter of months. Of course, that was several years past now and Eda wondered sometimes if she was doing the right thing staying on in Freshwater. The town just didn't seem to fit her anymore.

"Hey, you awake?" Suzanne called from the other side of the greenhouse. "You comin' to talk to me, or what?"

"On my way," Eda called as she scrambled to her feet. "I was just trying to maintain our sterling reputation for weirdness. Wouldn't want to disappoint anyone."

Her sad chuckle accompanied the sound of her steps across the brightly lit greenhouse.

CHAPTER SIX

The thick, heavy door to the Appledale Nursing Home opened as if it had twenty years' worth of grime encrusted between door and jamb. Kaylen pushed hard at the wooden monstrosity until it gave way with a disgusting, sticky sound. She stepped into the pale green hall that ran alongside a cluttered reception area to her right. Waving to the white-capped nurse reading at the front desk, Kaylen proceeded along the main hallway.

Chipped tiles underneath her feet often caught at her soles when she wore shoes with any type of heel. Today was bath day, however, and she had on her wide, square sandals. The uneven floor gave her no trouble as she moseyed along the maze of hallways to her father's room.

Joseph Royce Beale was a living example that it just didn't matter what you ate or how you lived your life, you could still live to a ripe old age. He had been raised on pork fatback, weed greens and gravy, with a few beans or potatoes thrown in now and then for good measure. At the tender age of ten, he began drinking hard whiskey, carousing with loose women, and smoking home-rolled cigarettes. He was now eighty-seven.

Today he looked good, his sun-abused skin holding good color and his hands steady. Some days he looked like death come knocking and those days scared Kaylen. Not because she was afraid of his dying, but because of how badly she wished he would die.

"Well, looka who's here," he said as he caught sight of her. "I din't know it was your day yet. How ya been?"

She pointedly ignored his good humor and, using the remote control on his bedside table, switched off the television.

"Hey, Daddy," she said finally. "How you feelin' today?"

Joseph studied her, his colorless eyes bleary and growing evil in his dark face. "Ain't you got yore ass on yore back. What's wrong with ya?"

Kaylen, busy fetching towels and clean clothes from the closet next to his tiny bathroom, didn't answer. She knew better than to tell him too much about anything.

Silence reigned as Kaylen briskly unfolded her father's wheelchair and pushed it to the side of the bed. Pulling down the sheet and thin blanket covering Joseph, she remained totally unmoved as his right hand crept up to painfully squeeze her left breast. Nonchalantly pushing his hand away, she twisted his frail form around and half-lifted, half-shoved him into the chair. A waft of sour body smell rose to her nostrils but she stoically ignored it and dropped the towels and clothing into his lap.

"I don't know why you don' love yore old papa no more, li'l gurl," he told her, shaking his head. "I been good to you all them years you was under my roof."

"That was a long time ago, Daddy," she replied, maneuvering the chair through the wide doorway and along the hall. "Now just hush and let's get this over with."

After they had traveled only a few feet into the hall, Joseph deliberately pushed the clothing and towels off his lap and onto the floor just like any misbehaving toddler.

"Damn you, Daddy. What is wrong with you?"

"I don't want no bath."

"Why not?" she asked, coming around to pick up the linens and clothing. Her voice was weary and subdued.

When he didn't answer, Kaylen tucked the clothing and towels awkwardly under her arm and continued to push the chair toward the bathroom. She was relieved to see the men's bath was unoccupied; she wouldn't have to wait with him.

The tiled room was large and efficient, with a deep, utilitarian tub that had plenty of safety guardrails for elderly people, as well as easy access via a hydraulic lift. There were also several showers with benches for the residents to use as they washed. Three lone urinals decorated a back wall and a rank of stalls with barroom doors stood to the left.

Kaylen preferred a shower usually for her father but decided to use the tub today, just for a change. Moving the chair close to the first wooden bench of the two that gradually descended into the tub, Kaylen used her foot to set the chair's brake then leaned to turn on the faucets. Joseph's hand shot out and fastened on her hip, working its way up under her T-shirt. After getting the water temperature right, Kaylen slapped his hand away and moved back.

"Behave yourself, Daddy. Don't you know how wrong that is?"

"Ain't nothin' wrong what makes you feel so good," he declared, smiling and showing dark vacant gaps where teeth had once lived.

"What if it doesn't make the other person feel very good?" she asked as she unbuttoned his pajama shirt. "You know why I have to come all the way out here and give you a bath, don't you? None of the nurses can stand to do it because you worry them so with your lecherous ways."

"They want it though," he said as if confiding a great secret. "Just like you do."

"Like hell," muttered Kaylen as she lifted him out of his pajama bottoms. She felt a twinge in one of her back muscles and knew she'd better slow down and watch her aggravation or she'd be sorry later.

After pulling his scrawny legs out of the pajamas, Kaylen swung her father onto the bench and pushed the wheelchair to one side. The tub was just about full and she shoved Joseph across the first bench onto the movable bench on the water side.

"Too damn hot," he told her as his feet sank in water up to the knees.

"Don't be so picky," she countered, "you've got to get clean and soap and hot water's the only way."

She moved behind him and thumbed the red button that set the hydraulic system into action. Slowly, with a grinding jolt, the bench Joseph sat upon sank with staccato jerks into the waist-deep water. Guilty, she double-checked to make sure the water wasn't too hot. It was fine, cooler than what she would have chosen for her bath.

Joseph squirmed as he lowered into the bath. His shriveled penis and testicles floated momentarily before disappearing under the water.

He complained during the entire bath, accusing her of trying to scald him like a pig carcass. He didn't like the way she scrubbed his back, his ass or washed his face. He accused her of tickling him on purpose when she tried to wash his feet and he deliberately tried to thwart her efforts at every turn. Once during the bath his flaccid penis hardened slightly and he grabbed it and shook it at her, asking her to look what a prize he had for her. She ignored the action.

Seeing the disparate parts of his manhood bobbing in the water made Kaylen think of old toys that resurface after many years. She thought of tiny teacups with the paint faded and scratched, twisted metal tricycles, broken Barbie dolls, and the toy that never really wore out—her father's penis. She remembered for the umpteenth time the first time he guided her tiny hands to this new and interesting toy. She had been amazed at how it could swell, practically on demand. And it also spit, a little at first then a lot later on.

She remembered the secrecy. She wasn't allowed to talk about it at school or to any of her friends. This was her private toy, he'd told her time and time again and if she told, they would take him away from her. Afraid, she hadn't mentioned it to anyone, not even her two older brothers. She often sensed they knew and even *agreed* with what he did to her. They never came right out and said it though, and she never asked.

Later she found out, from gossip shared by her friends, that this type of thing was wrong, dead wrong. Telling her father it was wrong hadn't helped. It actually made it worse because then he put the toy, with frantic, burning pain, through that between place in her legs, where fine hair was just beginning to sprout.

The fear of pregnancy shattered most of her teenage years, but it never happened. Not even later, when she was married to Chuck Stauder all those years.

Bent uncomfortably over the tub at Appledale, Kaylen thought of all those lost high school years and of its own volition, her hand tightened on the old man's scalp as she soaped his scant hair.

CHAPTER SEVEN

After leaving the spacious but poorly maintained grounds of Appledale, Kaylen drove her maroon Subaru along Freshwater's main street, reflecting that the town had changed little during the past twenty years.

Called Catholic Boulevard because of town founder Amos Freshwater's religious persuasion, the main street was narrow and winding, lined with ancient businesses that huddled together as if sorely afraid of the wide rural wilderness spreading on either side of the town.

Amos had been a miner for most of his life. Somehow—legend left a gap here—although he supposedly worked alone in the wilderness seeking his fortune, he managed to amass six wives and a passel of children. Tired of lugging miserable wives and uncivilized children through the mountains, he finally settled west of the Cape Fear River and used his hard-won earnings to establish the township of Freshwater. Soon there was a church, a school, even a bank, most of which catered to his now quite extensive family and their relatives.

Because many of his children were from a Cherokee Indian woman named Seishi and a few others by a Negro woman simply called Rim, the town passed an ordinance prohibiting discrimination within the town limits. Word spread and soon others came and settled in Freshwater to escape various prejudices in sterner localities.

You'd never know it now, Kaylen thought meanly as she drove south along Catholic. Bigotry and narrow-mindedness held the upper hand in modern Freshwater.

The decrepit stores and the wizened proprietors who manned them were pretty much the same as when she, as a child, had wandered this street more than thirty years ago. The clothing stores were still fly-specked, with faded samples of the finery of the past decorating the show windows. How many times had Kaylen, as a little girl, drooled over that polka-dotted blouse in Carmichael's window? Now the blouse hung limply, in ruined splendor, the bright red dots bleached until they almost blended with the white of the base fabric. The outdated shoes in the windows at Del Ekins store bore striped patterns of light and dark where the sun, year after year, had invaded through latticed windows. And no amount of coaxing could convince the adult Kaylen to eat one piece of the dusty, tacky penny candy from Andy Carter's Grocery though she had greedily consumed it by the handfuls when younger.

Kaylen had to admit that much of the fancy brickwork laid in the mid-1800s was lovely, especially the buildings of the wealthier merchants, the ones from old money, who had taken the time and trouble to maintain their inheritances. Viewed as a whole however, the town was a dying relic, filled with dying old people left behind by the younger generation who sought jobs and lives in nearby cities such as Raleigh, Fayetteville and Charlotte.

The town had seemed much older and even more dingy

when she had returned to marry Chuck Stauder after just a few years of college. And though it was her home, she still saw it as it truly was; a small insignificant town filled with busybodies.

She passed out of the town proper and headed south along state Route 24. Just five miles out and almost home, Kaylen pulled into the parking lot of Lerner's Grocery.

Built in the 1920s and remodeled very little over the years, Lerner's Grocery bore weathered wood siding of a nondescript beige color and a well-worn wooden interior. A BP Gas gondola decorated a solemn black post a few yards from the pocked and ruptured screen door.

Kaylen could have easily shopped at one of the regular supermarkets in Freshwater, but it just wasn't the same. The fluorescent lights puckered her eyes and the technological whir of computers made her nervous. Here she could shop in relative peace and, to her way of thinking, paying the extra, not-buying-in-bulk price was worth it.

Stepping inside, Kaylen felt comforted by the slapping squeak of an ancient and arthritis-stricken overhead fan. How she loved this old store with its smell of antiquity and its dusty shelves still bearing the popular fad items of a time long gone. The drone of daytime television was another familiar friend and Kaylen glanced briefly toward the checkout counter.

The cashier, Sharon Canody, *Mrs.* Canody to everyone who knew her, looked as though she had not moved since the last time Kaylen had shopped there, several weeks ago. She still sat two feet from a thirteen-inch color television, her chin propped in one pudgy hand. Continuously watching, every now and again she would blow a small pink bubble with the Bazooka bubble gum she invariably chewed.

Kaylen moved to the back of the store and rummaged through a large cardboard box filled with broken packages of office supplies. She dug patiently through loose pens, half-empty packages of erasers, paper clips, rubber bands, even batteries. Finally her fingers encountered treasure and she pulled out a partially crushed, but mostly intact, box of colored chalk.

Her movements then were precise and practiced as she gathered staples together—milk, bread, lettuce, whole-wheat flour (ordered and kept especially for her), several varieties of fruit, a couple packs of cigarettes and a bottle of salad dressing. Unable to remember what else she needed because, as usual, she hadn't made a list, Kaylen, arms laden, strode briskly to the counter.

Mrs. Canody rose slowly, like some great behemoth emerging from a mud playpen. The loose flesh of her bare arms swayed casually with movement as she passed each purchase along the counter and the topknot of dark hair adorning her wide head jiggled, seeming to laugh each time she chewed her gum. *It's like a perpetual motion machine*, Kaylen observed, much amused.

Magically, her eyes never leaving the television screen, Mrs. Canody managed to total Kaylen's order, even adding in the last-minute tabloid picked up impulsively, and make correct change from the money offered. It amazed Kaylen; had amazed her for years.

Only once in a decade had Mrs. Canody actually talked to Kaylen. With information gleaned from soap fan Delores Aldridge, who occasionally played cards with Kaylen's group, Kaylen had asked Mrs. Canody the right question: Would Luke and Laura get back together?

The response had been remarkable with Mrs. Canody actually looking at Kaylen and speaking.

"Oh, I definitely think so," she had confided in a gushing tone. "Those two were meant to be together as nobody else."

She had leaned close to Kaylen as if they were the best of friends. "Don't you think Luke is just the most beautiful man ever made? He's dreamy."

Kaylen smiled at the memory as she took her change from Mrs. Canody's outstretched hand. If only she knew more about soap opera stars, she could have had several meaningful conversations with the woman by now. Today, as usual, Mrs. Canody stolidly resumed her seat after she was finished with her duties. Her eyes never once lifted to Kaylen.

After leaving the store, Kaylen returned home, changed the clothing soiled by Joseph's bath and made a glass of iced tea. She took the tea and walked onto the wide front porch. Here there was a good view of Preacher's Haven, the largest mountain in this area, and the sloping mint green fields that cloaked the mountain's shoulders. Birds fluttered all around the house, wrapped up in their spring fertility rites.

Kaylen sank into a worn rocking chair and sipped daintily at her tea. Hours passed as she became lost in a familiar fantasy.

She is the only survivor of a horrible shipwreck. She and her sweet, anonymous lover had been traveling to Africa to sail up the Nile River, a trip they planned for many months. But in a small channel, just above the dark continent, a fierce storm gathered momentum and a freak wind had slammed their vessel into a stony embankment.

After floating for more than an hour, she washed up, parched and sunburned, on a sandy shore. Her lover is gone, and there is no sign of anyone else from the boat. But then hands are on her, soft, cool hands, flowing across her body as they lift her from the grating sand. Bright blue eyes, set in a blurred frame, gaze tenderly into hers. Such love is conveyed that it makes her heart lurch with something akin to pain.

The hands remain just a feather's breath away from tickling but the fleeting touch coupled with the passionate gaze arouses her body, igniting flame. The touch grows hot and her own hands flutter out seeking passionate perches of their own. Curves battle with angular planes under her questing fingers. Her previous lover is forgotten, wiped away by this new, intense being.

"I've been here a long time," a hoarse voice whispers close to her ear. "I've been alone. Now you are here."

"Yes," she answers against plump, burning lips, "now I am here."

A cool wind whipping across Kaylen brought her from reverie. A spring storm was brewing and she remained where she was, watching the clouds form ranks as if marching half-time into formation. Lightning danced and darted and wind abused the trees around her house. Within minutes huge raindrops began to fall and Kaylen, safely sheltered under the porch roof, watched the ballet of patterns they made.

Jarred out of her lethargy by the beauty of the storm, Kaylen wished desperately for something new in her life. Day after day her life fell into the same boring routines.

She had thought of remarrying after Chuck's sudden death from a heart attack but the selection of bachelors in the Freshwater area was unappetizing. She could choose between tobacco-chewing Pete Worsham or one-armed Roger Chowney, who people said was still crazy from the desert war. Schoolteacher Sid Thomas was another possibility, but she found his advances childish and disturbing. Truly, the whole thing seemed like too much trouble.

Since she had little interest in pleasing men or in fancying-up, and hated the cat-and-mouse flirting games, she was no doubt fated to spend the rest of her days alone. She wasn't overly disturbed by this notion; after all she had Jane Anne and the other ladies of the town to keep company with her. Nevertheless, it was a type of intimate, sensual companionship she really craved, perhaps someone to enjoy this storm with, to walk with, someone to sit with her when she had something to say. She desired intimacy, tenderness, qualities thus far lacking in her life.

Kaylen sighed and rubbed her palms along her crossed arms. She was sure about one thing, however; being alone could be preferable to marriage. For once she would like to have a relationship that did not revolve around someone else's needs. If she did remarry, she knew exactly what her part in it would be — cooking, cleaning, laundry and babying a man. And she'd had enough of that.

CHAPTER EIGHT

The letter had been short and sweet, endlessly recounting social events and coups that simply did not exist. But it was a letter her mother would like and approve and that's all that mattered these days.

Jane Anne scanned the letter one last time before sighing in frustration. She desperately hoped she had dropped no clue that her thoughts were less than charitable, her desires less than honorable. She licked the strip of adhesive and nervously pressed the envelope closed.

"Is that to your ma?" asked Mavis Dowd, her round, chubby face full of nosy friendship. "I was wondering what had happened to your letter this week."

"I've been real busy," Jane Anne replied, her smile polite but brittle. "We're getting ready for inventory at the library and you know that always sets me back."

"Don't I know it, honey. Seems like every other month or so, we got to be changing some kind of system in here just to stay with federal regulations, you know. Gets to be a pain."

Her pale hands fluttered with practiced accuracy over a stack of mail she was sorting into slotted bins.

"That must be rough," Jane Anne sympathized.

"How is your ma, by the way?" Mavis asked. "She get over that flu she had last month?"

"Sure. She won't let too much get her down, especially not something as nasty as flu." Jane Anne glanced out the large picture window, not in any hurry to get back to work.

"Did you hear about them Trimballs?" Mavis asked in a loud whisper. "I never heard of such before. And him a man with three children."

Jane Anne sighed, keeping her face averted from the postmaster. "Yes, I heard all about it."

Mavis sidled closer until only the counter and a few feet separated them. "I always figured them men like that couldn't, you know, do their husbandly duty, if you get my drift. You reckon them children are his? Maybe Margaret had a little on the sly, think so?"

"Could be, Mavis. They look like Ernie though, especially the oldest, Ben. Don't you think so?" Jane Anne said.

She was distracted suddenly by a flash of bright red paisley. A young woman had turned the corner from Court Street onto Catholic and was walking along the sidewalk. Mavis continued to talk in the background as Jane Anne leaned closer to the window to watch the approach of this interesting stranger.

It wasn't the clothing that drew Jane Anne, although the long, wildly patterned red skirt, brown sandals and muscle shirt marked her as one of the imports to Freshwater—one of the many groups of people who had established communities on the outskirts of the town. What fascinated Jane Anne was the young woman's breasts. They lolled beneath that sheer white muscle shirt, unbound and impudent, the visible dark areola and puckered nipples taunting Jane Anne.

The face too teased Jane Anne. The eyes sparkled with unspent mirth as they scanned the streets for new pleasures. Lips, naturally rosy, drew back from white, healthy teeth in a wide, unpinched smile, a smile that took in everyone and everything. *Come to me*, these lips said, *I want to talk to you, hear your story, tell you my story.*

Frazzled hair, the color of copper pennies, was drawn back into an untidy bun at the nape of the woman's neck as if declaring it was just too free to be properly tamed. Tendrils of copper ran riot, framing the woman's face in a Medusa coif.

"Well, would you look at that!" Mavis hissed just as the woman passed in front of the window and turned to enter the post office. She was preceded by a gust of sensuous patchouli scent.

Smiling at Jane Anne she inclined her head and gestured that Jane Anne could be waited on first.

"Oh no, I'm done," Jane Anne said quickly. "We were talking, that's all."

"Oh, okay, don't let me interrupt," the young woman told Jane Anne, as she began digging in her large woven handbag. "I know that letter's in here somewhere."

A cloaking silence fell as she searched, and hearing it, she lifted her head and studied the other two as her hand drew out an envelope.

"I only need to mail this," she said uncertainly. "It's okay, right? I mean, you aren't closed or anything, are you?"

Jane Anne shook her head and tried to put the girl at ease, a hard task with Mavis's disapproving frown glaring their way. "Not at all. You can lay it on the counter there."

The girl, a puzzled frown marring her wide brow, placed the sealed and stamped letter on the enameled counter. It lay there like a naked, abandoned infant. The three of them stared at it.

"Well, thanks," the young woman said finally. "I hope you ladies have a good day today."

Nodding at Jane Anne, she cast one more worried glance at

Mavis then left the small room. Jane Anne watched as she crossed the road, breasts chuckling gleefully beneath the thin shirt with each of her hurried steps.

Forestalling Mavis's certain comments, Jane Anne moved rapidly toward the door. "I've got to get back to work. You have a nice day, hear?"

Outside, in her truck, Jane Anne rested her forehead on the rim of the steering wheel and tried to sort out what she was feeling. The first and most obvious sensation was her traitorous body. Moist heat dappled her thighs and her upper chest and she found she was breathing in time to some strange throbbing that was shaking her body. Her hands trembled and she took them from her lap and placed them between her forehead and the steering wheel until the weight of her head quieted them.

Then her lap felt empty, bereft, and she pressed her legs together. This motion made her inner elbows caress her breasts on either side and she wanted to scream aloud at this new betrayal. Finally she threw her arms out wide and splayed her form across the seat. This was just as bad, with the coolness of air attacking her armpits, neck and groin.

She quickly sat up and turned the key in the ignition. If she could just get back to the library she would be safe.

Imagine the wanton actions of that woman, she fumed, showing her body in such a way! A woman like that is asking for trouble.

She realized she was thinking in the voice of her mother and she tried to push these thoughts away so she could find her own voice buried below. She wasn't sure, she conceded, that she would recognize her own voice if she did manage to find it.

She parked her truck in the library parking lot and sat still as stone. Focusing on the sensations of her body grounded her and helped bring her thoughts into focus. She had *liked* that girl! Had admired her strength, her honesty. Had wanted to be her, with her bouncing free breasts, her saucy hair, her long legs swishing against the ruffled paisley skirt as she proudly strode the streets of Freshwater.

41

Heart thumping loudly in her chest, Jane Anne knew she was going against everything she'd been taught all her life. A decent woman did not dress that way, not even in private. In the world of Jane Anne's mother, wives did not let their husbands see their breasts unbound. A true woman was always properly attired no matter her status. Even the necessary but evil act of procreation should be consummated under cover of complete darkness and half-dressed.

Jane Anne dropped her face into her hands, images of pink flesh on pink flesh capturing her mind. How she craved a lover, even though every previous, tentative attempt at sex had left her crestfallen and disappointed.

Her first lover had seemed nice enough, and was from a good family. They never talked of marriage, and it seemed like both knew the relationship would never amount to much. Then it was Christmas and they had gone to a party at the house of one of their friends. No parents had been anywhere about and it seemed as though disappearing into bedrooms was each couple's goal for the evening. And Jane Anne had gone along, too afraid of being different to protest. She had enjoyed the sleek sensation of lips and skin against hers but then had come that punishing shove and the unceasing drive to push, to enter, that made him ignore her pleas for patience, for time. And then that ultimate violation as he tore his way into her body, his drive never ceasing though she sobbed beneath him. Finished finally, he clumsily kissed her cheek and rolled away in search of another beer. She had lain there for the longest time, his spent passion oozing onto her thighs, mixing with her leaking blood. She'd felt so dirty, so used, she had vowed she would never again let someone control her in such a way.

This vow had been reinforced two months later as an Alabama physician scraped the last of this humiliation from its nestled place within her womb.

Jane Anne lifted her head and stared at the faded brick facade of the Freshwater Public Library.

And her mother had never known. A real victory, that.

CHAPTER NINE

Kaylen had decided, even before Chuck died, that she was going to have her yard professionally landscaped, one day contracting to have hundreds of flowers, trees and shrubs planted. She wanted her home surrounded by bright color all through the year.

Daily life had gotten in the way however, and then Chuck had passed, and the planting had been postponed, then postponed again. Finally, three weeks ago, when she had been cajoled into having her long gray hair cut and styled at Glory's Hair Salon, a bright green card had caught her eye as she waited her turn in Gloria's new state-of-the-art styling chair.

The card was hanging on Gloria's bulletin board amid dozens of others, but it called out to Kaylen. Long a believer in intuition and gut feeling, Kaylen immediately reached for it.

The small business card was a forest green color with a bright yellow sun decorating the upper left corner. *Helios Landscaping*, the card read, *Let us Brighten your Environment.*

Kaylen had smiled. The brightening of her environment was something she definitely wanted.

Kaylen went home and studied her new look with remorse. Before depression set in, she had called the number on the card.

A woman named Suzanne said she would send a design engineer to help Kaylen draw up plans for a new, aesthetically pleasing yard. But the company's engineer was busy on another job. Could Mrs. Stauder wait a week or two?

Mrs. Stauder replied that she had waited ten years. Two more weeks would not make a difference.

Unfortunately, Kaylen had forgotten to write the appointment down on her calendar—too busy mourning her lost hair—and she was trying to open a recalcitrant window in her living room when the engineer arrived.

Her house was about a hundred years old, a nineteenth-century frame farmhouse, and still contained many of the original multipaned windows from the 1940s. They worked about half the time, but Kaylen waxed optimistic and spent a lot of time babying them along during the spring.

The knock on her front door came at a crucial point, with her body pressed flat against the window as she gently rocked the sash to and fro to raise the pane.

"Goddamn it all to hell," she muttered as she bent her knees cautiously to make sure the heavy window wouldn't fall. Turning away from the window, she felt a hard tug at her waist and realized her T-shirt had become caught between window sash and frame.

Another knock sounded as she reached toward the sofa for a screwdriver that annoyingly remained just an inch away from her grasping fingertips. Her temper flared. "Who the hell is it?" she called.

"Helios Landscaping," was the reply from the other side of the door and memory came rushing back to Kaylen.

"I'm here," Kaylen called. "But you'll have to let yourself in."

The latch rattled open then and Kaylen breathed a sigh of relief. She turned back to the cotton cloth trapped in the window frame and began wagging it back and forth.

A sudden, enchanting giggle stopped her and she turned as far as she was able.

"I'm sorry, really, I didn't mean to laugh. It's just, you do look like you're in a pickle."

The lilting words issued from a tiny elf of a woman who had suddenly appeared in Kaylen's living room. A dark green T-shirt bearing the Helios sun logo, faded jeans, and a pair of grungy athletic shoes adorned a body that stood no more than five feet tall. She was young, achingly so, and watched Kaylen with frank green eyes, large in her small face. Her riotous mass of golden, sun-bronzed hair was caught back into an untidy ponytail, and her small, white teeth were just a little crooked in front.

This information washed over Kaylen in a drowning tide and she felt faint.

"Hey, are you okay," said the elf as she rushed forward to clap a hot palm to Kaylen's forehead. "You look a little pale. I really am sorry I laughed, I hope you're not mad or anything. Look, let me get you out of this mess so you can sit down."

With rapid, sure movements, the elf woman grabbed up the screwdriver and spread apart the inner window frame, allowing Kaylen to slump back and fall spread-eagled into an armchair.

The elf turned a concerned gaze on Kaylen and knelt down next to her. "Are you okay now? Do you want some water or something?"

Kaylen studied the unfamiliar face staring up at her and felt a strange shaking overtake her. Feeling foolish, she rubbed a hand across her face and smiled tremulously. "God, yes, I'm fine. You must think I'm an idiot."

The elf smiled, her crooked teeth endearing. "Shoot no, you were in a heck of a predicament. These old windows are a nuisance and a half. We had them when I was growing up and I can't tell you how many times I've pinched a finger in them."

The elf was so small, she moved in a blur of color. One minute she was at Kaylen's feet, the next she was at the window inspecting the sash and frame.

"You know," she began musingly, arms upraised to push against the sash, "these things have a counterweight. Do you know what that is?" She eyed Kaylen from under her outstretched arm.

At Kaylen's slow head shake, she went on. "Now don't get nervous. I'm gonna show you something but honest, I'm not hurting your house."

Using the screwdriver and a hammer Kaylen had left lying to one side, the elf began loosening the entire inner wooden frame of the window. A bit of plaster dust wafted down but her gentle methodology left the wall intact, even around the nail holes. Soon she had the inner frame on the left side loose enough to pull it away from the wall and set it aside.

Kaylen, who had not felt the least bit anxious during the procedure, could see the inner workings of the window then and she marveled at the innovation of those early builders. Rising to her feet, she moved closer.

"See?" said the elf woman, "this is how they work. This weight is attached to a rope which is attached to the window frame. When you raise the window the weight lowers and holds the window open. Pretty interesting, huh?"

Kaylen nodded as she examined the narrow chute that ran vertically alongside the window. At the bottom of the chute rested a thick sausage-shaped object made of metal, obviously the weight. At the top, a frayed rope swayed. The top of the rope had bunched up so Kaylen reached through cobwebs to pull it loose.

"See, what we need to do now is tie the rope back on the weight. If you have these old windows, you gotta know how to work on them because they come loose all the time. Even when my dad put metal staples on some of ours, on the rope, they still worked loose. Gravity's powerful stuff."

The elf woman worked as she talked, her small, strong fingers taking the rope and deftly wrapping it through a metal loop at the top of the weight and tying it in a practical square knot.

"Now," she said, stepping back. "Try to raise the window."

Kaylen obediently moved to push up on the bottom of the window. It moved up as the weight slid down. It was not as easy as a new window, because the many painted sides were swollen and grasping but it was much easier than before and required none of the usual strenuous rocking.

Kaylen smiled. "This is great! Look at it, it moves."

The elf woman smiled at Kaylen's joy then set about replacing the inner frame.

"Do you want me to check the other side of this one for you?" she asked when she had finished.

"No, no, you've done enough, I can check it later. Besides, I think this one's okay because it's going up so well. I'll check the others another time, the ones I have the most trouble with."

An awkward silence fell.

"Let's start over again," the elf woman said finally as she held out her hand toward Kaylen. "Hi, I'm Eda Byrne from Helios Landscaping."

Kaylen smiled in relief and shook the smaller woman's hand.

"Hi, Eda, I'm Kaylen Stauder and I'm the one who wants flowers in my yard."

Downing glasses of iced tea, spiced with fresh mint from the garden, the two women spent the next hour planning a whole new wardrobe for Kaylen's large yard.

Eda knew her business. With her small, tanned hands, she drew, using a sketch pad she fetched from her truck, precise, neat drawings from Kaylen's half-formed ideas. The drawings were to scale and Kaylen began to see exactly how beautiful her yard could become.

Pleased as she was, she was disturbed, however, by a strange inability to concentrate.

She would look sideways at Eda's fine head, tilted over the drawings with intense concentration, and her mind would begin to wander.

She admired the delicate line of Eda's jaw. The line appeared fragile, as if a swift blow would snap the girl's face in two, yet at the same time Kaylen could see the movement of strong tendons beneath the skin.

Sometimes Eda would sense Kaylen's interest and look up. She always smiled though, never seeming to take offense, and her eyes were merry. But Kaylen was embarrassed.

They walked outside together to measure the grounds before the drawings were complete. Eda not only praised Kaylen's vegetable garden but made suggestions on how to incorporate the garden into the landscaping plan by bordering the vegetables with flowers then branching walkways out from it.

It seemed a good idea.

"What about a line of boxwoods along the pathways," Kaylen suggested thoughtfully.

"Hmm, pretty expensive," Eda responded, "but if your heart is set on them..."

"No, no," she murmured.

"What about lavender instead?" Eda offered, studying Kaylen's face. "It's not as expensive and really looks nice as a bordering shrub."

Kaylen's mind filled with images of purple flowers. She smiled and nodded gratefully.

They walked on discussing types of walkways and Eda told Kaylen the choices: wooden planks, blocks or dowels, slate, brick, gravel, rock or wood chips.

Overwhelmed, Kaylen asked information about each type of material and discovered brick and slate both endured but could become slippery if wet. Wooden blocks could also become slippery and didn't last as long. She finally decided on white gravel with wooden framing. It was slightly more formal than wood chips but she felt it would better fit the vision of what she wanted.

The list of flower possibilities was endless and Kaylen had no real preferences or dislikes. Still having a hard time concentrating because of Eda's nearness, Kaylen finally threw her hands in the air and gave Eda *carte blanche.*

"Just order and plant whatever you feel would be nice. You know about plants and I don't," she told Eda.

Eda appeared to be more than surprised by this; her mouth hung open. "Are you sure? I mean my taste may be different than yours..."

Kaylen raised a hand, "Pish. I just want flowers and pleasant surroundings. Keep the cost within budget and I'll be content."

"Oh sure, I can do that and I'll even give you a firm estimate if you like before I actually begin work. That's no problem."

Deal struck, both turned in unison to walk back toward the house.

"By the way, who'll be doing the actual labor? Do you have a certain crew that works with you?" Kaylen asked as they neared the back steps.

"Well," Eda began with a sigh, "our business is run by women and we prefer women workers. We contract labor as needed. I hope that's okay."

"Oh, sure," Kaylen said hastily, "I was just curious. However you do business is fine."

A protracted silence fell as they entered the house, passed through the kitchen and into the living room. They paused before the front door.

"If you don't mind," began Eda in a soft voice, "I'd like to do a lot of the work on this project myself."

Kaylen swallowed once real hard, a strange sense of numbness creeping along her limbs. "Yes, certainly. That would be fine," she choked out.

"I mean, I like your grounds a lot, the way they're laid out and all. It's a real joy designing it and I'd like to make sure it's done right."

Eda raised her eyes and smiled at Kaylen. She opened the door and stepped into the bright sunshine. "Well, I guess I'll see you in a couple days, after I get the soil mix together."

"All right then," Kaylen said, raising her hand in farewell.

She watched through the screen door as the tiny elf woman slid into the small green pickup, with its yellow sun and company logo on the side, and pulled slowly onto Route 24.

Kaylen allowed the door to slip from her numb hands. She felt strange and didn't understand why.

Eda's face kept appearing in her mind, the large green eyes filled with merriment, the finely structured jaw, the pert nose —the combined whole of her. Kaylen had met pretty, even intensely beautiful women before, but none ever affected her in quite this way. This was more than mere admiration...or envy. It didn't sit the same.

Kaylen entered the kitchen and tried to concentrate on lunch. Nothing in the pantry appealed to her and she finally ended up drinking a tall glass of skim milk while standing at the kitchen sink. The milk assuaged her hunger yet didn't require her to think about preparation.

The rest of the day was spent cleaning house. She dusted everything to a glossy sheen and changed the linens on her bed. Her kitchen cabinets were cleaned out for the first time in years. The range received some much needed grease relief and worn sofa cushions were aired and fluffed. However, when she went to bed that night, bone-weary and work-sore, her mind fixated on the little garden girl. She forced the thoughts away but they drifted back.

Finally, she faced the issue and thought about Eda. She thought about her youth, her tiny delicate beauty. She wondered about the girl's history. Who were her parents? What were they like? Did she have brothers and sisters? Where did she go to school? Why did she get into landscaping as a career?

And most importantly, what did she think of Kaylen?

Weariness overtook Kaylen then and she fell into a fitful sleep, disturbed by vague dreams and confusing images.

CHAPTER TEN

The attraction was there. Eda felt it with every nerve in her body. Her veins sang as they transported blood under the thin sheath of her skin and each strand of her blond hair tingled as it moved. The possibility of falling in love inundated her, made her thinking fuzzy.

And this terrified her. Being so strongly enamored of someone—especially a straight woman she had just met—was frightening. She didn't know what to do, although hiding seemed like a good idea. She knew it would be folly to actively follow her inclination and try to act on the desire spawned from her short time with the Stauder woman. She knew the rule for women like her: never ever fall in love with a straight woman. She was supposed to stay with her own kind where things were slightly more delineated.

So, Eda did as she always did when she was troubled; she headed home.

Eda's parents lived north of Freshwater in a small ranch-style house. Compact, neat, constructed of weathered brick, the house had been a real challenge for Eda to landscape properly; too many plants would have overwhelmed the structure and too few would have left it entirely friendless. She had chosen a profusion of plants but used only lacy, open varieties such as wild rose, small papery daffodils, tall ethereal lilies and tiny-leafed willow trees. The overall effect actually enhanced the small, attractive structure.

Charles, Eda's father, drove eighty miles each day to work for the Budweiser brewery in nearby Greensboro. He'd done so for more than twenty years and had supported his family in modest comfort.

Eda's mother, Debbie, worked as a homemaker and she was there in the living room when her daughter arrived, her plump little feet plopped on a vinyl ottoman as she enjoyed daytime television. Sally Jesse Raphael's sympathetic voice cooed from the flickering screen.

Debbie Byrne had spent her entire life raising Eda and her two brothers and now, with one remaining almost-grown child at home, the laundry and cooking duties had diminished radically. Eda heartily approved of her mother's decision to watch morning TV in a ratty chenille bathrobe.

After a murmured greeting, Eda slid onto the sofa next to her mother's high-backed Queen Anne chair and focused on the program. Three women and two men sat side by side as the audience fired questions at them. It took Eda less than ten seconds to determine the show was about open marriages and that many of the people on Sally's panel had slept with other people on the panel with the full consent of everyone involved. The people in the audience were outraged and complimentary by turns.

"I just don't see how they do it," Debbie said finally. "Seems like they'd get it all confused."

Eda nodded and chewed on her thumbnail. "I suppose so.

Sexual attraction is a funny thing, you know?"

"Sex is a funny thing," her mother echoed in agreement. "Did you hear about Ernie Trimball?"

"Uh-uh. What about him?" She fiddled with the tangled lace of one sneaker. Unable to loosen it, she pried the shoe from her foot and used her teeth to work the knot.

"He's one of them queers too, or something. Dresses in women's clothes, or so I hear." Debbie lifted a mug off the small table next to her chair and took a deep sip of coffee.

Eda dropped her head and focused on the shoelace. This was exactly what she needed to hear today of all days.

"So how come I've never seen him prancing down Catholic in all his finery?" Eda asked finally, her tone just a tad belligerent. "Or seen him at the Frosthouse on gay night?"

Debbie looked at her daughter for the first time since her arrival. Eda cringed, knowing she probably looked frazzled, but she pointedly ignored vanity as she labored over the shoe.

"I guess he does it at home. Margaret told some of her friends at a card game the other night." She paused, still watching Eda. "Are you okay, honey? You seem like you might be upset about something."

Eda lifted her face and studied her mama's familiar features. Her mind flitted across the many times her mother had talked her through crisis after crisis; friends stabbing her in the back, teachers ignoring her exceptional academic effort because they thought she was cheating, and the death of a much loved pet. Could she tell her mother how the Stauder woman had affected her? Hell, she hadn't even really talked to her about Becca, or about Stephanie back in high school. The answer came to Eda with dire certainty. No. Debbie would never understand. Her scope was too limited. No matter how many talk shows she watched, no matter what gossip crossed her threshold, she just couldn't understand how one woman could be attracted to another with this hard, harsh longing. Compressing her lips together for a moment before answering, Eda finally reassured her mother.

"I'm fine. Starting a new job is all. You know how I get."

Debbie laughed and shifted her crossed ankles, seeking a better position. "Obsessed is what I call it. Who's the job for?"

"A woman named Stauder." Eda sighed, picturing the woman's face with its big, toothy smile and fine crinkles around eyes and mouth. "Out on Twenty-Four, south of town."

"That must be Kaylen Stauder. She's nice enough but kind of standoffish. Chuck, her husband, died a few years back. From what I understand she lives out there all alone."

Eda's ears perked. Kaylen, yes, that was her name.

"So she's good people?"

Debbie sighed and paused to watch a commercial for the best tea bag for iced tea.

"As good as most. Her father was a Beale from out Greensboro way, poor but churchgoin' folk. Her ma was one of them Bluefields from Raleigh. Big money, so I expect you won't have much trouble getting paid. I met her, the daughter, once at a church social. She's real nice but tall as a man. She wears funny clothes and all, too."

A wave of loneliness captured Eda and she found her attention wandering, leaping back to the time she'd spent with Kaylen. Debbie must have sensed Eda's lack of attention for she quieted and watched as a bald-headed health and fitness guru stir-fried vegetables on a new talk show.

Eda stood and stretched. "I'm goin' out back for a while."

Debbie nodded.

Eda moved toward the kitchen. Glancing at the stove she saw a pot boiling with a sluggish ill humor. The smell told her it was chicken and she wrinkled her nose in distaste. She never had liked her mother's chicken and dumplings and a sudden image of it on her mama's good dinner plates made her feel nauseated. Seeking fresh air she slammed open the kitchen door, pushed through the screen door and finally was free of the oppressive house.

A rough barnyard had been constructed in the small backyard by Eda and her brothers in an effort to hold the myriad stray animals they had brought home over the years. All three of them had been animal crazy since birth it seemed, although their mother had stated right off that all animals stayed outside. This iron rule had not been challenged, at least not that Eda could remember. So a passable barnyard, with fences and real outbuildings, albeit on a small scale, had been crafted by the Byrne children.

Eda remembered the time they had tried to keep an albino ferret, given to them by a friend, in the cage made to hold ducks and chickens. Terrified by the strutting rooster, the ferret had slipped through the coin-sized holes in the fencing time after time as Eda and her brothers rushed to get its smaller cage finished. Now, looking to her right, she saw the natural cul-de-sac made when the yard met forest, the place where the ferret was caught most often. Many a curse word had been uttered by her and her brothers and many a seriously scuffed knee had been suffered because of that little ferret. Eda remembered it as one of the best times of her life. Mainly because she and her brothers had forgotten their petty differences and jealousies in the mad scramble to save a creature they all cared about.

There weren't many animals here now; her younger brother, Tim, a senior in high school, was much too busy to care for the critters he once loved. Over a handful of years they had all died, whether from neglect or loneliness, Eda was never sure. Now only Hattie, an ancient German shepherd found at the dumpster in town when she was a puppy, lay snoozing in the sunshine flowing into the backyard. The few chickens her mama kept for eggs clucked concern from inside the ramshackle chicken coop and a tribe of barn cats called to each other on the still, spring air.

Eda walked across the yard, her tread slow. Studying the outbuildings, she knew many of them would not make it through another harsh winter and she felt a surge of sadness. It was strange how everything changed with time. It was as if all things weathered; wood, animals, relationships. Eda remembered well when her mother had seemed like the world to her. Now they had almost nothing in common.

Out of ingrained habit, Eda glanced about to make sure

no one observed her before sneaking into her favorite hiding place. And then she laughed at herself. Who cared, really, that she had this hideaway? Still, she thought as she shuffled into the crawlspace beneath her father's work shed, her arms flailing out in front to scare off spiders or mice, it was her private place and she didn't really want others to know about it.

She had almost outgrown the crawlspace, she realized with dismay. Even with her natural small stature, she still had to tuck and fold her legs in order to get them all the way inside. And then the space was cramped. She folded into a fetal position, her back fitting neatly into the curved banked dirt wall behind her. The view was the same; floorboards with wide cracks in between above her and red sandy dirt all around. Sunlight still crept in through the walls of the shed and filtered down through the floor cracks. She inhaled deeply, savoring the familiar scent of grassroot and dirt, leavened with the tang of oil and gasoline from her daddy's lawn mower.

Treasured possessions still lived in the crawlspace. The locket given her by Starla Jeffries was tucked, in its ancient fold-over baggie, beneath the wooden beam where wood met solid dirt. She remembered the day Starla had given her the locket, asking Eda to be her girlfriend. Eda had agreed, the pact sealed with a kiss, and they had been happy together, teaming up against the other kids in Mrs. Dollard's fifth-grade class, continuing together on through school through Mrs. Evan's eighth grade.

Eda recalled that glorious summer when their relationship had been in full bloom. Inseparable, they had explored almost all of Craig County together, irresistibly prying into the lives of all the adults they knew. She remembered the delighted ecstasy she had felt the first time they swam naked together in Friar's Creek. Sometimes, late at night, Eda could still feel Starla's blossoming body, wet slick, with cool and hot patches, as it moved against her own.

And there had been the laughter—a fine, natural laughter that had nourished both girls. Until it went away the day Starla was told they had to move north. Her dad, a career military man, was being transferred to Norfolk, Virginia.

Eda had been crushed and she remembered lying in this very place holding the weeping Starla in her arms, tears blurring her own vision as the slatted sun heated the air around them.

Would that relationship have weathered into dust? Or would it have lasted a lifetime?

Eagerly, Eda reached for the locket. Shaking off the dust, she pulled it from the bag. Moisture had gotten to it and the gold plated surface of the filigree heart was pitted and smudged with traveling metal. Opening it carefully, she lifted out the tiny slip of paper folded inside and gingerly unfolded it, her too-big fingers fumbling where once they had confidently tread.

Written inside, in loopy and rounded girlish letters, were the words '*I love you.*' The last message passed to Eda as the Jeffries family loaded itself into a wood-paneled station wagon.

Life had turned lonely for Eda after Starla had gone and she focused on her studies, grades soaring as animals became her best friends again. All relationships were avoided, though Eda's natural attractiveness made daily life at school a constant battle of wills when it came to boys. The wall of ice she maintained finally allowed her the safe freedom of solitude.

Eda decided she didn't really want to think about that time in her life. She wanted to remember the good times; like the time Starla had given her the locket. Eda studied the innocuous piece of jewelry, the pride of a young woman.

Carefully she refolded the paper and held it to her nose, hoping for the salty puppy-dog smell of Starla's hair when it was damp from the creek. She smelled only dust, and age. Sighing, she replaced the note tenderly into its locket home, the locket into the bag, and returned the compact little package to its niche.

Her thoughts fled to Mrs. Stauder—Kaylen—and the excitement this woman engendered in her. It was so similar to the protective tenderness and the quivering excitement she remembered feeling for Starla ten years ago. And different from what she had felt for the two other lovers since.

Eda laughed out loud for no real reason, the sound drawing

kittens which had been trying out new hunting skills nearby. One brave fellow answered the laugh with a loud meow as he peered at her from a narrow slit framed by wood and dirt at one long side of the crawlspace.

"Silly cat," Eda told him in a chiding voice. "Come around to the front so you can fit through."

The kitten, ignoring her advice and in his own bullheaded fashion, compressed his body and crept through the slot, tumbling down the short bank of dirt and coming to rest against Eda's stomach. He immediately leapt to his feet trying to maintain his dignity but only succeeded in shaking his body so hard he lost his footing again. Giving an indignant mew, he dug his claws into Eda's shirt and used it to crawl to her shoulder where he could once again be on top of his world.

Eda chuckled and further perplexed the kitten by shifting into a supine position and teasing him with her fingertip. He frolicked on her belly and she began to feel more in control.

This thing with Kaylen would just have to unfold as it would. She knew deep inside that agonizing over it wouldn't help, she merely had to have faith, and trust that things would click into place in a way best for her, and, she hoped, for all others concerned. Maybe she would be lucky. Maybe they wouldn't fall in love.

CHAPTER ELEVEN

Northside Elementary School was another Freshwater relic that would never change. The force of its sameness stunned Kaylen each time she stepped inside. There was a smell endemic to elementary schools—old food, book dust, chalk dust and the scent of hundreds of sweating children—and Kaylen inhaled deeply of this scent, so often touted in sentimental coming-of-age books, as she made her way down the central hallway. She actually didn't much like the smell. It reminded her of times best forgotten.

She was running a little late, having hoped to be at the school by nine thirty. She was suitably attired, in a modest, proper, flower-print dress. But she still wore her square sandals and figured that if anybody minded, they could look the other way. She really enjoyed the days she was asked to volunteer her time helping the children with various art projects.

The children. She peeked through the glass half of the door of Sid Thomas's first-grade class. The youngsters never failed to thrill her with their steady, no-nonsense gazes and their honest observations.

Sid, busy wiping childish graffiti from the blackboard, caught a glimpse of her out of the corner of his eye and rushed over. Flinging the door wide he eyed her appreciatively and smiled a smile that said the two of them shared a wonderful secret. Kaylen had yet to discover what that secret was, but found herself diligently pondering it each time they met.

Sid was a bachelor in his mid-thirties. Why he had never married was a real puzzle as he certainly was one of the handsomest men in Freshwater. He was a native of the town, the second son of Patrick and Weezie Thomas, who raised chickens for Holly Farms. Patrick had provided each of his four children with a college education and three of those children had gone on to have financially secure careers and loving families of their own. Only Sid had returned to Freshwater and begun teaching at Northside. He seemed to have a knack with children and the occasional rumors that questioned his bachelorhood status never affected his position there.

"Why, look who's here," he said loudly as he ushered her into his classroom. "It's Mrs. Stauder."

A well-rehearsed chorus of "Good morning, Mrs. Stauder" sounded out and Sid's hand dropped intimately into the small of Kaylen's back.

"Good morning, boys and girls," Kaylen told the rows of hastily scrubbed faces as she smiled widely and stepped forward. "And how are we this morning?"

Several children sang out "Fine" in answer and one little boy told her that his pet canary had died just that morning.

"Oh, I'm so sorry," Kaylen told the small freckled-faced boy. He had a charming cowlick in front, right atop his forehead. "Are you going to get another bird to help you forget this one?"

"I dunno," he replied with a shake of his head. "Mama says

she's glad he's gone 'cause he shit all over the place all the time."

After a few muffled giggles, Sid stepped forward. "All right boys and girls, Mrs. Stauder is going to do a new art project with you today. Let's all move to the art center so we can get started. Tommy, can you pass out those sheets of orange paper? Give one to everyone, yes, that's right."

He met Kaylen's disbelieving gaze and winked, smiling encouragingly. Kaylen began unloading chalk and geometric shapes cut from cardboard. An hour later, after each student had completed a picture of a chalk corona around the blankness of a geometric shape and had gone outside for recess, Sid and Kaylen relaxed together against the edge of his cluttered desk.

"That was a nice session," Sid told her as he fidgeted with a yellow pencil, flicking it back and forth between his fingers. "They seemed to enjoy it."

"Thanks." Kaylen could feel his eyes on her as she sat next to him, her eyes closed and her head thrown back. She heard him sigh.

"How come you never go out with me anymore?" he asked suddenly. "We used to have a good time."

Kaylen opened her eyes and turned to watch him as she answered, "I told you why."

"Because people were talking about us so much." He rose and moved to stare out the casement window. "And I told you I didn't care about that."

"Well, I care. We've never been...together that way, and I don't like people saying we have."

"But it's only speculation. Hell, life is made of speculation. It's what keeps us going. Besides," he turned to grin at her, "we can always flirt like mad and really give them something to talk about. It might be fun."

Kaylen had to smile in return. He was incorrigible.

"I'm sure you're quite the Casanova, Sid. I'm just afraid I wouldn't be able to keep up with you. I'm too old."

He laughed aloud and moved to stand in front of her. "Fuck the flirting, then. Let's just go out and have a good time. Wanna go see *ET* with me Saturday?"

Kaylen shook her head. "No thanks, Jane Anne and I went to see that movie last week. It's too sad." She paused. "I wish there were something different to do, some new place to go."

"How about that new dance hall in Sanford. Nobody's been there yet, it just opened."

Kaylen wrinkled her nose and sighed. "Can I call you about it later?"

Sid hung his head. "Yeah, that means you won't call. All right. I know when I'm beaten. Just tell me this. What do you want, Kaylen? What is it that would make you happy?" His voice deepened and lowered. "Do you have a lover? Someone out of town?"

Kaylen, thrown off guard by the question, had to fight a surge of indignation. "No, of course not!"

She thought a moment. "I don't know what I want. I want love, of course, but I also want a change. I want..."

She looked up into his candid brown eyes and felt at a loss.

"I'm not sure," she said finally. "I just hope I know it and enjoy it if I ever stumble across it."

The classroom door creaked open and the two of them were surrounded by a group of frenzied first-graders. There was a long disturbing moment however, when their eyes met and held, just above the bobbing heads of the children.

CHAPTER TWELVE

"I tell you, I knew it was coming," said Beverly Powell with a good dollop of self-righteous satisfaction.

"I mean you'd think they'd be using one of those raincoat thingies with all the fatal diseases bein' passed around nowadays."

The subject of discussion was young Penny Samples, whose pregnancy was finally beginning to show. Penny was the youngest daughter of Rea Samples, who worked as a nurse at the Amity Baptist Hospital about thirty minutes south of Freshwater.

"Well, she's been seeing that Ketchum boy from up on Cox's Creek for more than a year now," revealed Ellie Grayson in triumph. "I can't believe she hasn't been caught before."

She leaned forward and dropped her voice to an irresistible whisper. "You know all them Ketchums are trash, just trash. The mama even smokes cigars...in public!"

This last was delivered with such a flourish that it made even Kaylen's stomach lurch. In what? Distaste? Excitement?

An afternoon meeting of the Freshwater Magnolias was just coming to a close. The Magnolia club had originally been formed five years ago to raise money for the oldest Withers boy, who, at the time, was undergoing expensive cancer treatments at a big northern hospital. And although the Withers boy had passed on, succumbing to the rare bone cancer, the group continued to meet once a month like clockwork. The meeting sites varied; today they had gathered at the local rural electric cooperative building on Catholic Boulevard.

The group did contribute to good works, including numerous fundraisers to help the general community. Now averaging about ten members, Sully Peters the most recent to be embraced, the continuance of the club was really to provide an excuse, under the guise of civic duty, for these women to escape their routine lives and discuss the latest news. The annual ten dollar dues seemed a small enough price to pay. Kaylen Stauder wasn't thrilled with her membership but figured it was better than sitting at home watching the philodendron grow.

Jane Anne seemed in a cool, distant mood today. She hadn't said more than a few words to Kaylen and even less to everyone else. This was unusual, for Jane Anne could always be depended upon for the light chitchat that kept these social gatherings moving smoothly. People were noticing too, as Kaylen saw many a pointed glance directed toward her friend and a lot of sly whispering and nudging going on.

Leaving the ooh-so-glad-it-wasn't-me discussion of Penny's condition, Kaylen moved across the room and cornered Jane Anne as she was dipping up small paper cups of sherbet punch.

"Hey, gal, how's it hanging?" she said to Jane Anne, trying to meet her eyes.

Jane Anne favored her with a cool stare and answered with words shrouded in chipped ice. "By a thin thread and an unraveling knot."

Kaylen gave a low whistle. "What happened?"

"It's that shit at the library," Jane Anne said haltingly.

"Saints preserve us," Kaylen mocked with twinkling eyes. "Let me go home and write this in my diary. I need to remember the day Jane Anne said the word shit."

Jane Anne eyed her with frustrated impatience so Kaylen backed off and dipped fingers into the salted peanuts piled into a small china dish.

"So tell me," she said finally, chewing the nuts loudly.

"Oh, it's David again. I swear every time he comes near me in the library, I just cringe. I'm either going to have to find another job or just raise a ruckus."

"I vote for raising the ruckus," Kaylen said, reaching for the pastel-colored pillow mints.

"You would. I'm just not confrontational about things, you know that." She dabbed her hands on a paper towel, then folded it neatly and rested the silver dipper atop it. "I really like the man, but he is a sexual predator. But I'm sure he doesn't mean anything by it."

"The hell he doesn't! He'd nail you in a minute if you so much as nodded his way."

"But he's married," Jane Anne protested.

"Even more reason to do the nasty with you. All men like a little on the side, or so I've been told. Are you going to tell his wife?"

"I don't know. Kit is such a dear and I enjoy working with her so much..." Her voice trailed off, it too quailing in indecision.

"You need to do something. You've been putting up with his groping for years now." Kaylen took a cup of punch and drained it in two swallows.

"I know it," Jane Anne hissed angrily.

"Go on and sleep with him one time," Kaylen advised calmly, studying her friend's reaction. "If you do that I can almost guarantee he'll leave you alone. He may want one or two more couplings but then he'll wander off looking for a new conquest. Trust me." She nodded as if all the wisdom of the ages rested on her slim shoulders.

Jane Anne's mouth hung open just a bit. "I can't believe you, Kaylen. Do you lie in bed at night and think this stuff up?"

"Well, what have you got to lose? You might even enjoy it."

Jane Anne picked up the dipper and began stirring the punch with uncommon vigor. "Why do I even talk to you?" She paused in her stirring and glared at Kaylen. "I could lose a lot. My job, my reputation, and besides..." She lowered her eyes to the punch, yet taking a foolhardy leap. "He's not exactly my type, if you know what I mean."

"What's not to like? He's handsome, well-built, he adores you. That's everyone's type."

Jane Anne hung her head and shook it back and forth, her eyes closed and her pinned-up, schoolmarmish bun jiggling. "You just don't get it, do you?"

Kaylen fiddled with her lace collar, scratching inside where it itched. "Get what? Am I missing something?"

"No, no."

Jane Anne busied her hands with the cake, arranging the slices in a perfect slant formation. Silence stretched between them with a backdrop drone of women's voices as the other members gossiped across the room.

"Look, is something else wrong?" Kaylen studied Jane Anne, honestly worried about her closest friend. "You can tell me anything, you know that."

"It's silly."

"Jane Anne, I never think of you as silly. A pain in the ass maybe, but never silly." She smiled and Jane Anne blushed and returned the smile briefly.

"It's just...you said you'd call me about cards last night. I waited up until eleven."

Kaylen smacked her forehead with the heel of her hand. "Damn! I knew there was something I was going to do. I forgot it completely. I'm so sorry."

"Well, it's all right. I went ahead and renewed that book for you, the one about African jewelry. I didn't hear from you last night, whether you'd finished it, and it was due."

"Thanks, I appreciate that. I'd owe my life savings in fines if it wasn't for you."

"Don't keep it too long though, that hippie girl from Cypress Flats is waiting for it."

"I won't. I'm pretty much done with it." Kaylen heard the voices moving closer and saw that they were going to be besieged by Magnolias from all sides. The food was out and the word had passed.

"Cards tonight?" Kaylen whispered just as Ellie Grayson made a dive for the punchbowl.

Jane Anne nodded and smiled. Her mood was much improved. All the Magnolias remarked upon it.

CHAPTER THIRTEEN

David and Kit Baker worked with Jane Anne at the Freshwater Community Library, a tall and ugly brick building at the northern end of Catholic Boulevard. Nobody knew what the building had been originally, although many believed it had been used as a hospital during the War Between the States. Some said it had first been constructed as a Baptist church, simply because it was built at the far end of town, away from the primarily Catholic community of Amos Freshwater's time.

The Bakers had been with the library since it had been taken over and run by the town council, David returning books to the shelves and acting as all-around handyman, and Kit working as assistant librarian. Even after more than twenty years' service, neither had moved up the ladder of succession. Both seemed content, working alongside one imported librarian after another.

With her experience, Kit could have been head librarian many times over, but each time County Administrator George Adams mentioned promoting her, she threatened to quit, stating ambiguously that one librarian was as good as another. She often declared she was just fine where she was as long as the town hired someone pleasant for her to work with. Branded an eccentric and so humored, her wishes were complied with.

Jane Anne couldn't remember exactly when David had become obsessed with adding her to his list of sexual conquests. She had thought him a wonderfully distinguished older gentleman, frankly admiring his stately bearing and calm demeanor when she'd arrived five years ago, but to this day she did not believe she had led him on in any way. From local gossip, she gleaned that he'd hit on or slept with most of the women in town and that his poor wife Kit was seen as one of the most long-suffering women in the area.

Jane Anne wondered at this description because to her Kit appeared one of the happiest women in town. There seemed to be no schism in the marriage either, the two of them acting like young teenagers in love when they thought they were unobserved. Jane Anne often innocently entered in on a playful sex-oriented scene between the two: the tweaking of a buttock cheek, the sensuous tongue kiss, or even the surreptitious zipping of trousers. She often felt as if the library storage room was actually a bed just waiting for something to happen. David seemed to want her to climb onto the bed with him too and, who knew, maybe even with Kit, for just a little frolic. His hands were always on her in one fashion or another and Kit seemed blissfully unconcerned. Involvement with David Baker was something Jane Anne definitely did not want.

Now, commiserating in Kaylen's spacious kitchen, she felt hard-pressed to list her reasons for avoiding it. Fear kept her silent, however, afraid she'd distance her best friend forever.

Kaylen definitely was not her usual sympathetic self toward Jane Anne's plight and after again encouraging her to go for the sexual gusto, she abruptly changed the subject.

"I'm finally having my yard landscaped," she announced while dealing cards for rummy.

"Landscaped? You mean like graded? Dug up?" Jane Anne queried in surprise.

Kaylen lit a cigarette and waved the smoke away. "No, just planted with flowers and stuff. I don't think they'll have to move much dirt. The yard's pretty level."

Jane Anne nodded. "Who's doing it?"

Laughing, Kaylen told her about the arrival of the little elf girl, Eda, while she was stuck in the window.

"I'd probably still be hanging there if she hadn't gotten me loose," she concluded.

"And she knew how the windows work in this old house?" Jane Anne placed her elbow on the table and propped her chin in her hand.

"Yeah." Kaylen shrugged. "I've already gone through and taken them all apart. It really makes a difference when you hook the weights back up to the ropes. I can't believe I was too dumb to figure it out all these years."

"Seems like Chuck would've known too."

Kaylen nodded absently as she pondered the fan of cards she held.

"So when are they going to start work?" Jane Anne asked, watching avidly as Kaylen laid down a trio of threes and a jack, queen, and king of hearts.

"She said she'd be back in a few days when she had some soil ready or something like that." Kaylen sat back, drawing on her cigarette, clearly gloating over her card-playing skill.

Not to be outdone, Jane Anne grinned in glory as she laid down three aces. "What all are you going to have done, exactly?"

"Just some pathways, gravel, with flower borders, then some circle gardens scattered here and there. I may even start that herb garden I've been talking about." She drew a card from the deck, discarded, then nodded as a signal for Jane Anne to play.

"That'll be real pretty, Kaylen. How long does this girl expect it to take?" She drew a card then laid down three twos.

Kaylen studied the cards spread out on the table for a good long while. Silence stretched taut as Kaylen drew and laid down the six through nine of clubs.

Jane Anne sighed in appreciation and, after drawing, played her own set of fours before discarding.

Watching, a slow smile of mischievous glee curled Kaylen's features. "Ain't you just dying to know how much it'll cost?"

Jane Anne, still lost in thought, looked up in surprise. "What?"

"The yard job. Don't you want to know how much it'll set me back?"

Jane Anne shook her head and sipped at her iced tea. So much water had condensed on the outside that it dripped all the way to her mouth. After taking a deep sip, she fetched a paper towel from a nearby counter and mopped at her dress and the table.

"Well?" Kaylen persisted.

"Kaylen, are you sure you're southern bred? I know you didn't have the benefit of a mother, God rest her, but didn't you have anyone to help teach you manners? Southern ladies just don't speak of such things. Plain and simple. It's rude to talk about how much things cost."

"Oh, for Christ's sake. Next you'll be telling me I should never wear white shoes before Easter, no matter how nice the weather and when it's my turn to serve the punch at the next Magnolia meeting I'd better make damn sure my dress matches the color of the punch." Kaylen twirled her iced tea glass back and forth, enjoying the tinkling of the ice. Strangely enough, it made her think of Eda's laughter.

"Well." Jane Anne shrugged and laid down three kings.

Kaylen glanced at her own hand and moaned, quickly re-evaluating her moves.

"A proper southern lady just knows these things, Kaylen, without thinking about it."

"Your mama must have Chattahoochee River water running in her veins, that's all I can say," murmured Kaylen as she laid down an ace, two, three run.

"Now, don't get started on my mama again," Jane Anne warned ominously.

"She's too, too southern," laughed Kaylen with an apologetic demeanor. "I bet she can trace her family back to when the first convicts came to Yamacraw Bluff." She snickered into her tea glass.

"Yamacraw Bluff?"

"Savannah, you know," Kaylen explained.

"If my mama could hear you, ma'am, she'd wash your mouth out with soap so quick." Jane Anne rummied the four and five of clubs on Kaylen's cards and laid down three fives.

Kaylen laughed and laid down the ten, jack and queen of spades. "I ain't afraid of your mama."

"You should be, everyone in Atlanta is." Jane Anne grinned and laid down three sixes and the seven, eight and nine of spades.

"You know, I think this Eda person is pretty neat. Imagine, working as a landscape engineer. It sounds so...creative maybe?" Kaylen rummied the four of spades on her partner and laid down the ten, jack and queen of clubs.

Jane Anne, slightly miffed at having their playful sparring interrupted, replied quietly. "It sounds like hot, dirty work, fittin' only for white trash types." She laid down the seven, eight and nine of hearts and discarded the ten, promptly going out. "Ha! I bet I won."

After a long moment of silence, she looked up to see Kaylen staring at her with piercing brown eyes.

"What?"

"Don't go calling people white trash when you haven't even met them yet," said Kaylen firmly. "I think she's nice and there ain't nothin' trashy about her."

"Lord, Kaylen, I didn't mean anything by it. I was just mouthing off. Why are you so sensitive all of a sudden?" Alarm etched itself on her fine, softly aging features. A frown darkened her dusky blue eyes.

Kaylen began gathering the cards together, not even counting points to see who won. "I'm sorry. I've been on edge lately for some odd reason."

Jane Anne smiled her relief. "You're probably tired of Ellie's mouth. I swear I think she took the hide off everybody in town today."

"The woman does have a mean mouth on her. Isn't that a shame about the Samples girl though. Babies having babies. It's just too much."

A truce had been declared, of sorts, but the two friends decided against another hand. It had been a long day. Jane Anne left and made her way home before ten o'clock.

CHAPTER FOURTEEN

A few days later, early in the morning, when Kaylen opened her kitchen door to see how her garden grew, she heard an odd humming sound. Listening intently as she sipped her coffee, she decided it was a person humming a tune...and the tune sounded like the refrain from Jethro Tull's *Aqualung*. Smiling, she listened a bit longer. Yep, she was able to hum along.

Retreating to the bedroom, she added a pair of shorts to the T-shirt and panties she'd slept in then retraced her steps and went out the kitchen door. Rounding the side of the house, she discovered Eda sitting on the ground, her back propped against the young magnolia tree in the north yard. She held a sketchbook in one hand. Several oversize rolls of paper lay at her side. Sketching, lost in thought and humming intently, she didn't hear Kaylen's approach.

"Well, hello," Kaylen said several minutes later, just as Aqualung was picking up a dog end. Eda looked up and smiled. Kaylen noted her green eyes seemed smudged with shadows and a small scratch had appeared on her chin since she'd last seen her. Otherwise she looked the same, with her wild blond hair piled into disarray on the back of her head instead of pulled back into a sleek ponytail.

"Hey, how are you this morning? I hope you don't mind me coming out so early. The gals are bringing the dirt out about nine and I wanted to make sure these plans were finalized and approved before they got here."

"Sure, that's okay. Come on in the house and have some coffee while we talk about it."

Eda gathered her things and stood, brushing off the seat of her khaki shorts. Inside the kitchen, Kaylen motioned for Eda to sit at the table as she turned to the coffeemaker. By the time she turned back around, full coffee mug in hand, Eda had spread out the plans, very similar to blueprints, on the kitchen table.

"There's sugar and milk," she told Eda as she handed her the coffee.

Eda accepted the cup and wrapped both hands around the mug as if the warmth was a pure, sensuous thrill. "I like it just like this." She blew on the surface of the coffee a few times then took a cautious sip. "Mmmm, that's good. What kind is it?"

Kaylen smiled, glad someone else appreciated her eclectic taste in coffee. "It's a French blend, expensive as hell but I figure if I'm going to drink coffee, which everyone tells me is so bad for me, I'm going to drink coffee. Know what I mean?"

Eda's frank, unswerving gaze, over the rim of the coffee cup, met Kaylen's then and Kaylen suddenly felt that strange tingling she'd felt the first day they'd met. Her throat began to close and she felt as if she might drown. The racing tempo of her heart as the adrenalin of fear pumped into her system allowed her to finally break the eye contact.

"I know exactly what you mean," Eda said.

Did her voice tremble slightly? Kaylen wondered. Seeking

control, Kaylen glanced at the overlarge sheets of paper spread on her table. "So the plans, are they finished then?"

"Mostly." Excitement lit Eda's voice. "Tell me what you think."

Kaylen moved closer to study the drawings. They were neat and precise. A large rectangle labeled HOUSE dominated the center with a smaller rectangle above it labeled GARDEN. Branching out from the garden and extending around to other rectangles on either side of the house were walkways with a ninety-degree angle where they turned from backyard to side yard. Two large circular areas dominated the front yard on either side of a wide walkway leading to the front porch.

Eda leaned forward and with a slim, callused finger began highlighting certain points.

"I thought we'd go with marigolds bordering the entire garden, except where the walkways join. Marigolds come in so many colors and are really good for keeping insects away during the growing season. Do you like marigolds?" She eyed Kaylen expectantly.

"Yes, yes I do," stuttered Kaylen.

"Good, because I also put them as borders around this garden," she pointed to the south side yard, "and the flower garden here." She pointed to the northern side yard. "I thought I'd plant lavender bushes all along the two walkways leading from the vegetable garden, with a redbud tree in each elbow of the walkway on the house side. I'll probably put some of those grassy-type daffodils under each tree so you'll have a little color there until the trees bloom."

"This is incredible," Kaylen breathed. "How did you get all this planned out so quickly?"

Eda laughed her tinkling laugh. "Darlin', I'm good," she joked. "Seriously, I got inspired and couldn't put the plans down. It's been a lot of fun for me."

"And this is all within my budget?"

"Yeah, pretty close. Suzanne, my boss, the gal you spoke to that first time? Well, she has greenhouses and if we get the plants through her, they'll cost a lot less. The trees I'm gonna have to buy from a woman in Raleigh but she's given me good prices in the past. The lavender is going to be the bitch—sorry—the problem, because it takes awhile for the plants to grow into shrubs. If we buy them the correct size, it'll cost a good bit. If you buy the young plants from Suzanne though, you'll save a bundle."

"How will it look," Kaylen asked, head whirling.

"Well." Eda sighed and sipped her coffee. "Not as nice. I won't lie to you. But they will bloom some the first year. What you'll have essentially is small dark plants lining the walkways, no taller than say, a daffodil. If you keep them trimmed right and if all goes well, in several years they'll be shrub size and nice and woody."

"So you think I should get the young plants?"

"Yes, I do. Why pay three times the price just because the plants are older?" She turned toward the coffeemaker. "May I get another cup of coffee?"

"Sure, help yourself," Kaylen answered absently, attention fixed on the drawings. "What's in the circular gardens on the front lawn, I can't make out these names," she asked a moment later.

"Oh, some are in Latin. Those are dwarf willows surrounded by a circle of marigolds then a circle of chrysanthemums. We can define the circles in brick like most people do, but short railroad ties might be more in keeping with the rest of the plan."

"And up here by the house?" Eda materialized next to her as Kaylen pointed to two rectangles, one on either side of the wide front door.

"Those are azaleas," explained Eda. "I thought some color up against the side of the house might be a nice touch."

"And these are daffodils and tulips along the central walk?"

"Yeah," Eda replied, sipping noisily at her coffee. "With crocus and grape hyacinths added in. I figured we could layer so there would be some flowers up until midsummer. Even then you'll still have some greenery there."

She paused to look up and study Kaylen's face. "So, what do

you think?"

Eda's close proximity was making Kaylen feel strange, actually uncomfortable. The tingling feeling was back as well. Many incoherent thoughts chased themselves through her mind. She wondered whether Eda would notice how the weak, flabby skin beneath her chin and along her jaw was sagging. Did she smell okay? She hadn't yet showered.

Slowly she lowered her eyes to Eda's upturned face. Eda was watching her, eyes clear and direct. She seemed to study Kaylen, seeking to fathom her very being.

Kaylen was slammed hard by a crazy desire to kiss Eda. She wanted to press her own lips against the weathered ones below her. She fancied she could already taste the warm, coffee-scented breath as it fanned into her mouth. The fragrance of clean, sun-heated skin assailed her nostrils and she quickly averted her eyes and her face, realizing how dangerously close she had actually come to trading spit with another woman, for God's sake.

She moved away as tactfully as possible and refilled her cup as she tried to get her shaky emotions under control. "You know, you have done one hell of a job," she said finally, her back still turned toward Eda.

"Do you really think so?" Eda asked. She strode across the kitchen so she could see Kaylen's face. "You like all of it? There's nothing you want changed?"

Kaylen smiled at her enthusiasm. "Yes, I really do. It's exactly what I had in mind."

"Sheesh!" Eda exhaled and let her back bump against the edge of the counter. "That's such a relief. I'm always so nervous when I show someone one of my designs."

"No! Not you," Kaylen exclaimed. "You seem cool as a cucumber. You sure fooled me."

Eda shrugged and screwed her features into a knot. "It's the image, y'know. I gotta do a good job for Helios. Be professional, and all."

"You are a professional. No one could do a design like this and not—"

Kaylen was interrupted by the rumbling sound of a large truck pulling up outside. Eda slipped her cup into the sink and ran out the back door with Kaylen following at a more sedate pace.

A large dump truck with dusty sides sat in Kaylen's drive. The driver, a young, sturdy woman, slightly older than Eda, stood by the open truck door talking to Eda. Every now and then the driver would slap her billed cap at the leg of her dirty coverall, sending clouds of dust billowing. They talked for some time before walking over to Kaylen.

"Mrs. Stauder, this is Cathy, one of our workers," Eda said over the low drone of the truck's idling engine. "We were wondering where we could pile the soil mix until we use it all."

Kaylen leaned to shake Cathy's hand but was deeply disturbed by the huge slashing scar that bisected Cathy's lean, otherwise lovely face.

"Well, how much soil is it?" she asked after a minute of perplexity.

"Hmm, it'll be at least two truckloads but the pile will go down all the time as we use it."

Kaylen shrugged. "Where do you think it should go, Eda?"

Eda smiled her understanding. "Lots of decisions for you, aren't there? Maybe close to the house here on the right. Not too noticeable, but close to where we're working. I plan to stretch a tarp over it but it won't look too bad. Is that okay?"

Kaylen nodded gratefully and Eda bestowed her with a quick but brilliant smile. She swung herself up into the truck cab next to the other woman.

Kaylen spent the rest of the morning watching the two women in action. They were efficient and Kaylen marveled because all this efficiency was being generated by females. Not that females weren't capable of efficiency: she had long believed that women could do almost anything men did, usually better and faster. It was just nice to see her beliefs manifested in real life.

A huge mound of dark, loose soil was dumped at the side of the house and Kaylen was situated so she could see the two women on the truck shoveling off the last bit that didn't slide off. After neatening the pile a bit, Cathy drove the dump truck away and Eda drove her own smaller truck around and unloaded all sorts of tools and implements, including a wheelbarrow which seemed too large for her to handle. Eda hummed as she worked, every now and then pausing in midstride to give Kaylen a little smile of exuberant joy.

Kaylen began to feel embarrassed that Eda was noticing her so often so she went inside to shower and dress. Just as she emerged from her bedroom, ready for the day, the telephone jangled. Jane Anne, asking her to go shopping.

"I can't today, Jane Anne. Eda is here working on the yard," Kaylen told her.

"So, how does it look? Different?" Jane Anne asked, her tone light.

"All I have right now is a big pile of dirt. That Eda is something else. You should see what she has laid out for my yard, all sorts of flowers and trees."

"Umm hmm," Jane Anne agreed quietly. "I'll look forward to seeing it when it's finished."

"Yeah," Kaylen joked, "me too, if I survive all this change in my life."

"Well," Jane Anne reminded her, "you've been saying you wanted something different, so here you are."

They signed off after agreeing to meet later in the week and do something together.

Kaylen went into the kitchen and made a stack of cucumber sandwiches—store-bought but still good—and glasses of lemonade. Adding potato chips to the plate as an afterthought, she carried the tray outside.

Eda was bent over the outside spigot rinsing off her hands as Kaylen rounded the house.

"You must've read my mind," she exclaimed when she caught sight of Kaylen and the tray. "I was just gettin' ready to slip down the road and grab a bite."

Kaylen smiled sheepishly. "Well, now, I don't know good this is but it'll fill you up, I suppose."

They ate together in the shade of a ragged magnolia tree, talking easily about vegetarianism—neither of them cared much for meat—and about whether or not an Arkansas governor would make a comeback as president.

Kaylen spent the afternoon weeding in her garden as Eda measured out the new garden lots and marked them with wooden stakes and baling twine.

Kaylen, too frequently, stopped what she was doing and stared with rapt attention as Eda's tight, economical form worked. Kaylen felt confused.

CHAPTER FIFTEEN

The library was unusually crowded and normally this upsurge in literary interest would have pleased Jane Anne. Today she wished for the power to blink her eyes and make all the people disappear.

She felt perilously close to crying.

Angered by her emotional weakness, she focused all energies into her work. But then there came the time when everyone had been checked out, books had been replaced, and the Bakers had left the building to go to lunch. Jane Anne was suddenly all alone with her traitorous thoughts. Damn Kaylen!

"*I can't today, Jane Anne, Eda is here.*" The words resounded with mocking weight in her mind. She had never suspected that Kaylen would prove to be so fickle. Imagine pulling away from her just because, well, because this Eda person was working on the yard.

Suppose this was merely an excuse to avoid spending time with her? Suppose Kaylen had figured out how her best friend really felt about her? Suppose Kaylen hated her now?

Jane Anne took a deep breath and tried to quiet her rioting mind. Surely, being adults, they could work this insanity out. It would be a relief, really, if Kaylen knew how she felt. Then it would all be over with and the issue would be resolved—whether for good or bad.

Jane Anne walked out of the main reading room and into the long dark hall that led to the ancient bathrooms. Just outside the ladies' room, she bent and took a deep pull from the water fountain, her blue eyes lifting to the poster on the wall just above. *Foster the Love of Reading!* it proclaimed in big bold letters. The photo artwork showed a mother holding a small girl. They shared a book between them but the mother was watching the daughter with a look of tender fondness.

Disgusted, she turned away and entered the ladies' room. She needed Kaylen today, damn it! This was the day of her mother's weekly phone call and she was not sure she could handle it the way she felt right now.

She leaned against the wall next to the bathroom basins and closed her eyes, trying to imagine a life without Kaylen. The image hurt so badly that her eyes snapped open and breath hitched in her throat.

She tried to remember what life had been like five years ago, before Kaylen had staggered into the library with that huge stack of books, and found it no longer existed. She had nothing in her life but Kaylen. If Kaylen was lost to her then she would die. Her life would wither until there was absolutely nothing left.

Moving to stand in front of the mirror, she assessed herself harshly. Tall, skinny, almost no breasts or ass; who was she kidding? Why would anyone want her? Her face was okay, a bland normal, but her hair was mousy and graying, dead looking. She heard her mother's voice:

"You've got to use that rosewater soap, Janey, or you'll have crocodile

skin before you're thirty and who'll want you then?"

And from Thanksgiving three years ago;

"I don't know why you don't use some of that Clairol color on your hair, Jane Anne, or at least one of those henna shampoos to give that hair of yours a little life. God, you look like one of those bag ladies downtown."

Jane Anne slammed her fist on the side of the enamel basin.

"No!" she said aloud. "Shut the fuck UP!"

Swiveling away from the mirror, she rested her back against the chilly tiles of the wall. She shut her eyes and called up a familiar fantasy.

She is with Kaylen. They are having tea in Kaylen's living room when she abruptly sets her cup on the coffee table, stands, reaches for Jane Anne and pulls her to her feet. Her hands caress Jane Anne's face and her lips conquer Jane Anne's mouth, dominating her completely, leaving her weak and breathless. These same lips travel down, leaving moist trails along Jane Anne's neck and suddenly bare shoulders. Jane Anne feels herself pressing her breasts to Kaylen, trying to crawl inside her skin. Kaylen draws her close, a strong hand cupping one buttock as she grinds their lower bodies together.

"I love you," she whispers tenderly as her mouth travels lower and lower. Jane Anne's breasts swell and tingle in anticipation...

"Oh, my God," Jane Anne whispered, pulling her shaking hands away from her own body. She came back to awareness with a jolt, realizing where she was and what she was doing. She turned to the nearest basin, refusing to look at her reflection in the mirror. She stood there for more than a minute, panting, trying to get her breathing under control.

The heavy door to the ladies' room opened with a rude shriek and wizened Peggy Harper entered. Jane Anne whirled to face the elderly lady and worked hard to recall how to offer a smile that wasn't a grimace of pain and shame.

"Mrs. Harper. How are you today?" she gasped.

Peggy, grandmother to the shrewd and nosy Ellie, displayed

the family trait. "You sick?" she grunted in her peculiarly irritating voice. "You look like you're sick."

"No, no, felt a little dizzy is all. Just came to get a splash of water," Jane Anne replied hastily.

"Ummhmm," muttered Peggy in a speculative manner.

Jane Anne realized suddenly that the woman thought she was pregnant!

"It's just the dust from the books, Mrs. Harper, really. I have a slight allergy to the dust."

Moving to one of the stalls along the far wall, Peggy watched Jane Anne suspiciously. "Seems a bad choice, librarian, if you're allergic to books, don't it?"

After the sharp rustle of nylon, the sound of loud voiding echoed in the bathroom. Jane Anne quickly switched on the hot water tap and began scrubbing her treacherous hands, fighting the tears lurking just behind her eyes.

Peggy joined her at the next basin, washing her hands and wetting a dirty plastic comb that she ran through her short, steel gray hair. Wet trails of darker hair made her head look like a cornfield. An image of green stalks of corn atop of Peggy Harper's squared and blocked head appeared in front of Jane Anne's eyes.

Jane Anne realized she might be losing her mind.

Quickly, she finished drying her hands and dropped the brown paper towel into the waste bin. "Well, back to work," she said cheerfully, adding silently that if she really was losing her mind, she might as well enjoy it.

"I guess so. We was all lookin' for you, you know," Peggy snapped, eyes accusing Jane Anne.

"I know," Jane Anne said sympathetically. "I didn't mean to be so long."

Fighting an urge to bite the woman, Jane Anne held the door for her. Peggy dropped her own paper towel and with a condemning sniff hobbled past on her swollen ankles.

CHAPTER SIXTEEN

The next day Eda worked alone, outlining the flower plots with string and using crosses of wood to mark the location of various solitary plants and trees.

Kaylen cleaned house, every now and then pausing to marvel at the younger woman in action. Eda was full of energy, brimming with the cherished vitality of youth that older people lost as they neared the dreaded middle-age stage of their lives. It saddened Kaylen to watch Eda, knowing she could never recapture that essence at this point in her life. She began to feel old and useless.

The sky started to darken and by noon a spring thunderstorm had set in. Kaylen fetched Eda and brought her inside to eat lunch and wait for the storm to pass.

Lunch was salad greens from the garden, crispy fried potatoes, and last year's canned peaches with whipped topping as dessert. Eda thoroughly and obviously enjoyed the food and Kaylen watched in amazement as she packed several helpings away.

"You like to eat, don't you?" she said finally, amused.

Eda, caught off guard and made self-conscious, answered slowly. "Oh, I'm sorry. Mama always said I wasn't fit to eat in polite company."

"Don't be silly. I like seeing someone who knows how to enjoy food. I can't help but wonder where you put it all."

"I guess I have a hollow leg," Eda said with an apologetic smile. "I eat this way all the time. Mama says I'm just hoping I'll grow some more and get bigger. I never do though." She ingested another large forkful of potatoes.

"You mind if I smoke?" Kaylen asked, politely holding up her cigarette pack.

"Not if you don't mind if I eat," Eda countered, motioning for Kaylen to go ahead.

Kaylen sat back in her chair so she wouldn't be blowing smoke directly at her. "Tell me about your mother. What's she like?"

"Well," Eda replied thoughtfully, "she's short, like me, but plump and full of piss and vinegar. My daddy's a big ol' man but he jumps when my mama says jump. My brothers do too."

"How many brothers and sisters do you have?"

"Just brothers. Two. Mean as snakes, too. They got the tallness and the meanness and I got the shortness and the stubbornness of the family."

"But ya'll get along?" Kaylen handed Eda the bowl of salad so she could get a third helping.

"Yeah, we hang out together when we're all home, but Jeffrey works as a lawyer in Raleigh now and Timothy is just finishing up high school here in town. He's dating and all, too."

"Jeffrey's married?"

"No, not yet. He's engaged to Karen, though, and they'll be getting married in a year or so. She's trying to get her degree in elementary education."

"What about you? Aren't you going to college?" Eda quit chewing suddenly and Kaylen felt a shiver of alarm creep through her.

"Now that's a touchy topic," Eda said finally, with candor. "Especially with my family. See, I've got one of those photographic memories, you know, where I learn really easily? It allowed me to graduate high school with honors. I was offered a couple scholarships but I just..."

She paused and fiddled with the collar of her T-shirt. "I don't think I'm ready for college life."

"Why? Because you're...what? Short?" Kaylen frowned, trying to understand.

Eda laughed. "No. Well, maybe. Mama thinks it's that too. She says it was a shame I didn't get my daddy's height instead of hers. Of course, it's not that. I just don't think...I mean I'm wanting to do something else. Believe it or not, I love what I'm doing right now. Planning beautiful places for people has always intrigued me. And I am a licensed landscape architect. I've been doing it four years now and haven't tired of it yet."

"Think you'll go to college later?"

"Oh, probably. My scores are really great so I feel like I'll have no trouble getting in a few years from now. And I have money saved up. I'm not worried about it. Do you think I'm crazy?" She fixed her clear gaze on Kaylen.

Kaylen shrugged and took her empty plate to the sink. "The way I see it, it's your life and you have every right to live it as you choose. Be happy. Life's too short."

Eda was at her side in an instant and she wrapped one strong arm about Kaylen's waist and gave her a hard, quick squeeze as she placed her own plate into the sink. "Thanks, Mrs. Stauder, you're the sweetest thing."

Kaylen, nonplused, murmured, "Kaylen, please call me Kaylen."

Eda stepped back and looked up at her. "Are you sure? Thanks, Kaylen."

They cleared the table together in silence, the patter and slap of the rain on the soft soil outside the only cadence. Realizing the rain wasn't going to let up, Kaylen suffered a mixture of emotions. She wanted Eda to stay with her, but she felt odd asking her to stay. And she felt odd wanting her to stay so badly. She craved some type of intimacy with this small, bright woman but was totally confused by this desire. Also what form did she want this intimacy to take—emotional, physical, intellectual, spiritual? Did she want Eda to become the child she never was able to conceive?

She looked up and studied Eda who was bent over the sink washing their few dishes in a fog of soapsuds. She even washed dishes intently, giving the menial chore her total concentration.

What was it about the young woman? What drew her? Was it that intensity? Her small elfin form? Or maybe it was her quick, agile mind. Or perhaps it was just her natural air of happiness and contentment. Kaylen had never met a person put together quite so well emotionally.

Kaylen sighed as she put the last bowl of leftovers into the refrigerator. She had no clue. She only knew that Eda coming into her life had had a profound effect on her and thoughts of her populated her mind day and night. It was disturbing.

"Hey, do you play rummy?" she asked when they were both drying their hands on tea towels.

Eda looked up and grinned as if relieved. "Rummy? It's my life. I learned it at my grandma's knee, so you'd better beware."

"You're forgetting something," Kaylen reminded Eda as she retrieved the cards from their carved wooden box beneath the window. "I've got years of experience on my side."

"Hey, age doesn't matter. Besides, you old people always forget things and..." Eda paused, a horrified expression on her face and her body froze in mid-movement.

Kaylen knew what had happened. Eda was afraid her simple joke had offended her. Somehow Eda had sensed her turmoil about her age and was afraid there would be some sensitivity about mentioning it. Kaylen, with all her middle-aged wisdom, knew she meant no harm.

And she suddenly realized Eda did not really think of her as old. Otherwise, she would never have dared joke about it in such a way. Sudden warmth suffused Kaylen and she smiled, determined to put Eda at ease.

"Who are you calling old, you little twerp. Just because the body has a few miles on it doesn't mean the mind isn't still sharp. You just wait and see." She nodded sagely as she took her seat at the table. "I'll show you how to play rummy."

They played hand after close hand until almost dinner time and as Eda left the house to make her way home along the rain dampened roads, Kaylen felt a great sense of loss seize her heart and make her tremble.

"It's just like being in love," she mused in puzzlement, as she closed and locked the front door.

Erotic dreams plagued her that night. A silk-clad Eda moved sinuously through a Middle Eastern dance featuring seven veils. Kaylen woke as one of the silky veils left Eda's body, baring it, and came to waft gently across Kaylen's brow. Disappointment swamped her as she opened her eyes to a dark, empty bedroom.

CHAPTER SEVENTEEN

Joseph was in a foul mood the next morning when Kaylen visited him. He scowled when she said hello, resisted all her attempts to undress him, and even threw a bar of soap that hit her on the cheek.

"Godammit Daddy, who pissed in your Cheerios this morning?" she asked through gritted teeth as she retrieved the soap from the floor of the men's bathroom.

"You just get yore ass on back home. You're useless, good for nothin'," he told her, his mouth working tired gums.

Kaylen tried to placate him. "Now, Daddy, you don't mean that. I thought you liked having me come down here and take care of you."

"Harrump, who's been fillin' yore head with foolishness. You ain't worth a damn, never was. Pukey, whiney li'l gurl, then grew up an' married a fool. Hell, you couldn' even have me some granchildern. Now what use is that?"

Anger gripped Kaylen in a tightening web. Her hand shot out and fastened on the old man's chin and she turned his bony, speckled head around so she was looking directly into his bleary, washed-out eyes.

"Look here, old man, I don't want to hear any of your trash today, hear me? Either you do what I say or I'm turning your ass around right now and taking you back to bed. The only reason I take care of you is because the good book says you're to respect your parents. I don't do it because I like it."

Joseph's eyes grew mean. "Listen to you, talkin' to yore poor ol' daddy thata way. Ungrateful gurrrl, that's what you are. Ungrateful, unnnnnnnngrateful!" He pounded the arm of his wheelchair with one balled up fist, the cords in his neck standing out and his face reddening.

Hot damn, maybe he'll have a stroke, Kaylen thought meanly. She thought of Jane Anne then, and knew she would be horrified by Kaylen's thoughts.

Quickly making a decision, she gathered together her father's clean and dirty clothes into an untidy ball and wheeled his half-naked form from the bathroom and out into the hall. He immediately stopped yelling and began saying "Wha'? wha'?" in an astonished tone.

Elderly residents watched them with jaundiced eyes and slack jaws as they passed by wheelchair after wheelchair on the way to Joseph's room. Kaylen had had just about all she could handle and a great sense of freedom washed over her. She didn't have to come here and take his abuse once a week. She and her brothers made sure Appledale was paid to care for her father. If one of the attendants couldn't bathe him then he could simply stay dirty. There was just too much muddy water between her and her father.

She lifted Joseph to his feet and unceremoniously dumped him on the bed and roughly fastened his pajama trousers. She didn't bother replacing his shirt, instead she just pulled the blanket up and tucked it in under his scrawny arms.

"Kaylen? What're you doin, li'l gal? Ain't you gonna give yore papa a bath?" His tone was childlike, wheedling.

"No, Daddy, I'm not. You can just lie there and stink the rest of your life away for all I care. I've put up with your mouth and your filthy hands on me for too damned long." She fetched up his clothes and threw them into the chair by the window.

"I'll stop in next week and see you and I'll sit right over in that chair just prim and proper as can be. A southern lady visiting her father. I will not bathe you and I will not feed you." She rubbed her cheek, still stinging from the impact of the bar of soap. "Goodbye Daddy, I'll see you then."

She paused outside the door to his room, chest heaving, and leaned against the wall, eyes closed, calming her anger. When she opened her eyes, she was looking into the rheumy gaze of a very old woman who was sitting in a wheelchair in the hall. The woman reminded Kaylen of Eda, somehow, with her direct stare and no-nonsense air. Placing her gnarled hands on the oversize wheels of her chair, she nodded her approval to Kaylen and wheeled her chair slowly into the room directly across from Joseph's room.

Later, at the library, she shared her victory with Jane Anne.

"It felt so amazing," she said as she twisted the shoulder strap of her backpack. She was leaning over the checkout counter, her feet now and then lifting from the floor as she shifted her weight to the counter. She felt like a child of ten instead of a woman who'd reached the middle of her life. "I especially liked the look on his face when I wheeled him from the bathroom."

Jane Anne was trying to understand but Kaylen knew she felt her friend had gone too far.

"Are you sure this is what you want? I sure wouldn't treat my daddy that way. What about all those years he took care of you? And without a mother for ya'll too."

"He took care of me all right," Kaylen replied sarcastically. "Look, you don't know that whole story. A lot of stuff happened when I was young that just wasn't right and—"

"Well, all children have spats with their daddy, that's part of growing up," Jane Anne said sensibly as she checked in a pile of returned books.

"You sure know how to bust someone's bubble, Jane Anne. I swear I don't know why I hang out with you."

Jane Anne smiled, a move that transformed her drawn, schoolmarm face into a face of rare beauty. "Because I'm just so adorable, you can't stay away?"

Kaylen propped her chin on the heel of her palm. "Something like that. When can you leave? I'm hungry."

Lunch was at their usual place, Paddy's, a small restaurant on Catholic Boulevard which specialized in home cooking. It was operated by Patty Campbell, whom Kaylen had gone to school with when Patty still weighed a mere two hundred pounds. Patty now weighed in at close to five hundred. She could for sure cook and Kaylen and Jane Anne had never had a bad meal at Paddy's.

Today they both had soft hot rolls, mushroom barley soup and warm apple cobbler. Patty came over to sit and talk with them for a short while, her chins waggling with each word, but hurriedly lumbered off when an ominous crash sounded from the kitchen.

"I sure would hate to get on the wrong side of her," said Kaylen to Patty's retreating back. "I feel sorry for whoever messed up in the kitchen."

"She's really a sweetheart though," stated Jane Anne. "Hey, how's your yard coming?"

"Oh, it's wonderful," Kaylen sighed. "I'm going to have tons of flowers and trees. You name it, I think Eda's going to plant it." She munched on a crisp piece of crust.

"And Eda, are you two getting along?"

"Of course, why wouldn't we? She's amazing. I've never seen anyone work as hard as she does, and she seems to enjoy it, which is what blows me away. You should come out and watch her sometime."

"Watch her?" Jane Anne lifted a brow in surprise. "I don't

think so. I'd be embarrassed just standing there watching someone work."

"Oh, she doesn't mind. I do it all the time."

Jane Anne strangled on her iced tea, causing Kaylen to look up in bewilderment.

"You do? Why?" Jane Anne asked when she had caught her breath.

Kaylen felt a blush beginning but forced herself to relax and remain cool. "Why not? It's interesting." She bent to her cobbler.

"What's she like, this Eda?" Jane Anne turned her attention to her own plate.

Kaylen chewed as she thought. "Well, she's real small, has lots of blond hair. She has pretty green eyes. And she's smart, even winning lots of scholarships."

"But she works as a landscape engineer?"

"She says she likes it," Kaylen explained with a shrug.

"It couldn't pay that well."

"I don't know, she's certified and says she's able to save money."

"Well, where does she live?"

"Hmm." Kaylen screwed up her nose. "I don't know, I've never asked. She's real close to her family so maybe she lives with them. I really want the two of you to meet. Maybe we can all get together for dinner sometime."

"Sure. Whatever," Jane Anne said without enthusiasm.

Kaylen pondered her friend and suddenly realized that maybe Jane Anne thought their friendship was in jeopardy, that Eda might take Kaylen away somehow. She was just about to reassure Jane Anne when Ellie, Beverly and Jeanie entered Paddy's. They had their gray, curly-permed heads together and were whispering animatedly. Jeanie spotted Kaylen and Jane Anne and the trio moved as one toward their table.

"Well, look who's here," said Ellie, pulling a chair from the next table and settling heavily into it.

"And what are you ladies up to," asked Beverly with mock

slyness.

Kaylen laughed and lifted her dish as evidence. "Eating, Beverly. It is lunchtime."

Beverly made a face then turned her attention to Jane Anne. "Did you hear about David?"

Jane Anne shook her head. "No, what?"

"Word is he's sleeping with someone from over Eastside," whispered Ellie, her eyes wide. Jeanie shivered with delight and Kaylen eyed her disdainfully.

"So," sighed Jane Anne, "who is it this time? Someone we know?"

Ellie, Jeanie and Beverly looked at each other and snickered gleefully. Jane Anne's and Kaylen's eyes met and Kaylen winked.

"It's a man," blurted Beverly in a stage whisper.

Jane Anne drew back in shock. "No way. He likes women, I'm sure of it."

The three newcomers grew silent immediately and stared at Jane Anne, eyes rabid with the possibility of new blood.

"And just how do you know so well?" Jeanie finally asked, her sparse, graying mustache twitching under its covering of face powder.

"Don't worry," Jane Anne assured them, "I'm not having an affair with him. You can just tell he and Kit are...well, are very attracted to one another."

"That may be," Ellie countered, "but Mac Markel was delivering nabs over to the vendors at that park over at Eastside and he saw the two of them together. He swore to me they were holding hands and one time they even went behind the bathroom wall and kissed. Tradin' tongues too."

"I don't believe this," Kaylen said. "How could Mac see?"

"He was right there at the vending machine, just beside the bathrooms," Ellie said defensively.

"Well, didn't David and this...person, see Mac?" Jane Anne asked.

"No, they went on in the bathroom together. Mac said he waited a while but they didn't come right out and he had his work to do," added Jeanie.

"He swears it was David though, all dressed up too, just like he usually is."

Silence descended as each woman pondered this new knowledge.

"Well, ladies, hello. Can I get you something for lunch today?" Patty had come up behind them and was waiting with pencil and pad poised.

"Why, yes, thank you, Patty," Ellie said sweetly.

After each lady had ordered however, and Patty had shuffled off, the three immediately began talking about Patty's size and how she hadn't yet paid her personal property taxes for the year.

After just a few more minutes Kaylen and Jane Anne excused themselves. Kaylen drove Jane Anne back to the library. They were strangely silent the entire way, just murmuring a subdued farewell at the library's back entrance.

Driving home alone, Kaylen felt sorrow sweep through her. She had liked David and felt sad that he would be forced to leave Freshwater.

CHAPTER EIGHTEEN

Eda and her crew were still working outside when Kaylen returned home after lunch with Jane Anne. Still saddened by the news about David, Kaylen didn't spend much time talking to the women but retreated into the sanctuary of her home after a brief hello. After preparing herself a cup of hot chamomile tea to settle a stomach set abroil by the news of the day, she curled up on the sofa in her living room and fell into escapist fantasy.

She is an artists' model from the 1920s. Her slim form is dressed in a soft, flexible sheath, her hair wrapped and oiled as is the custom of the time. The model is naked beneath the tight dress, her privates moist and expectant, making her inner thighs uncommonly wet as she walks along the sidewalk. She is checking the house numbers of the high, clustered homes along the Rue de Delasser. She glances again at the slip of paper in her hand, even though she knows the numbers have not changed since last she looked. As she climbs the narrow, cramped stairway, which smells of dust and old food, a baby cries somewhere above her and a woman sings along with a scratchy recording cylinder somewhere below. The keening sound of the song oppresses her and she pauses a moment to listen, to experience the sadness fully.

But he awaits and she climbs again, thoughts and premonitions of the afternoon bouncing in her mind. What will he expect from her?

They had met at a party, one held by Cerisse Lavan at her sumptuous rooms at the Hotel Grande. The model's body suddenly remembers the way he'd cupped her buttocks in his hot hands. He had come up from behind as she stood slanted in a doorway, his strong patchouli scent inundating her, then his hands had been on her, his low, rich voice sounding in her ear.

"You are so lovely, so slender but richly curved. I must paint you. Will you come to me?"

These had been his first words to her. Later, they had been introduced and she had learned where he lived and that he was indeed a painter of high repute. He knew she had been working as a model for many months, padding her meager earnings by writing for two local publications. He told her he enjoyed her work, all the while lowering his hooded eyes to scan her form.

At the top floor she waits to catch her breath and adjusts her clothing. She isn't nervous, only excited and aroused. He opens the door shortly after her knock and sweeps her immediately into his arms.

"Cherie," he says, sweeping her round and round. "You came to us as I knew you would."

She gasps for breath as he releases her. "I received your missive only two hours ago. I am sorry for the delay."

"Not to worry, we waited for you. Come, there's wine and fruit. Are you hungry? Thirsty?"

We? She looks about and spies a tiny woman reclining on a divan. The painter's easel has been set up nearby and all seems in readiness.

Upon closer examination, she sees the woman is very lovely, with a small pointy face and deep, green eyes, large in her smallness, and a heavy cloud of dark blond hair that reaches to her waist. She is dressed in a robe of fine Chinese silk, sumptuous with red and gold embroidery.

The painter hands the model a chilled glass of pale wine and leads her to the divan. "This is my wife, Eva. Is she not lovely, too?"

The model nods and extends her hand. "Eva."

"Hello. Welcome to our home." Eva's eyes glow with warmth as she takes the model's hand and pulls her down next to her. The painter then addresses the model.

"Today I will paint you and you will write about our time here. I have read your work and find it a melody to the senses. Your words are like poetry and magic and Eva and I want them to be ours."

The model watches him in total confusion. "You want me to write for you? I thought you wanted a model."

"I do," he says quickly. He anxiously paces the worn floorboards of the studio. "We have our own private collection of canvasses and of writings. These works are not for public display because the material could be considered rather...shocking, even in these modern times. We wish you and your work added to this collection and feel you could truly appreciate what we are doing."

The model sips her wine hastily as her mind studies the information.

"Are these works of a…" She pauses and her tongue moistens her lip. "A sexual nature?"

"She is sharp, Eva," the painter tells his wife. He turns and moves closer to the model, "I will pay whatever you ask, a modeling fee as well as a fee for each story you write for us. This seems more than fair."

The model, amazed at this generosity, is also amazed when Eva's tiny hand begins touching her back in fleeting caresses which send shivers through her. Her voice is shaky when she speaks.

"Yes, yes, more than fair."

"Well done. My agent will visit you in the morning with the necessary papers. You just tell him the figure and he will write it in. No questions asked."

He lifts a splattered smock from a straight-backed chair behind the easel. "Now we will work, and play."

She rises and turns to study Eva who is still half-reclining on the satin divan, her robe parted and showing short, sleek legs. Smiling into

Eva's eyes, she reaches around to unfasten the back of her dress. She has unfastened the first four hooks when Eva pulls her arm away.

"Here, let me help you," she says, drawing the model to her side. Her nimble fingers soon have the garment loosened and her eager hands sweep over the model's soft, pale skin. Eva's lips follow her hands until it seems flames of fire replace the trail of moisture from her mouth. The soft dress falls, revealing the model's small, pointed breasts and slim waist. Eva cups her breasts from behind, murmuring loving phrases into the model's ear.

Sensation swamps the model and she feels her regular world dropping into oblivion as she steps into this new place, full of familiar but not familiar tastes, smells and touches, the intensity of each causing her to almost swoon yet remain alert for fear of missing any part of the experience.

A knock on the kitchen door sent Kaylen tumbling head over heels back into reality. She was shaken and shocked by her daydream, wanting to feel disgust but feeling a strange elation instead. The knock was repeated and she heard Eda calling her name through the screen door. Trying to gather her wits, Kaylen rose and stumbled to the door.

"Hey, Kaylen, were you asleep?"

Kaylen smiled mistily, the pleasure of the fantasy lingering. "Well, sort of."

"Hmmm, by the look on your face, it looks as though the dream was a good one." Eda smiled.

"It was good. Come on in and have a glass of tea or something to eat," she said, holding the door ajar. Eda shook her head sadly. Her look was hangdog as she glanced up at Kaylen. "I'd better not. I promised Molly I'd give her a ride home. Everyone else is already gone."

"Oh, all right." Disappointment stabbed at Kaylen but she managed to smile. "I guess I'll see you tomorrow then."

Again Eda shook her head apologetically. "No, I've got to run into Raleigh tomorrow and pick up the trees. The girls will still come over and finish that back left walkway if that's okay."

"Oh, fine, yeah. I'll..." What could she say? She decided honesty was best. "I'll miss you though."

Eda's face brightened and her eyes met Kaylen's eagerly. "Really? I'll miss you too."

Awkwardness reigned, neither woman knowing what to say until Kaylen said, "Well, I'll see you the day after, I guess."

"I'll bring some nice trees back for you. This woman has some real pretty ones." She turned to walk away, glancing back once to wave.

"'Bye, Kaylen."

"'Bye, Eva," Kaylen said softly.

A moment later her eyes widened in horror and her bare toes curled on the cool kitchen floor. She had called Eda Eva. And, to add to the horror, the Eva of her daydream had looked identical to the Eda of real life, albeit more relaxed than Kaylen had ever seen Eda. It was at that moment that Kaylen realized she was deeply, physically attracted to another woman. She could already feel her whole world crumbling about her shoulders.

CHAPTER NINETEEN

Disturbed and afraid, Kaylen spent the next twenty-four hours reliving her past, seeking signs that indicated she was one of those "lesbian women." What being one of "those women" actually entailed she wasn't sure, but felt the trait should have been obvious sometime in her past. After all, people always talked about one person being this way and another person that way.

Men who were homosexuals were effeminate and affectatious and women homosexuals always wore boots, leather jackets and cropped their hair ridiculously short.

Or did they? Kaylen had no real criteria for judging.

Still she didn't feel as though she fit the "gay" stereotype. True, she never wore heels as other women did, always opting for comfortable shoes, and hiking boots on occasion. And true, she didn't wear makeup, even to church and especially since Chuck's death. She had never been one to polish her nails or run to the beauty salon each week. But she always attributed these things to being a tomboy and now getting older and not caring about her appearance as much.

She thought of all the lesbians she'd seen—precious few in her life. There had been a few couples at college. Activist women, always ready to march against something. Kaylen did look more like them, especially now that her hair was short, but she had no desire to march anywhere. Was that a requirement?

But what about the way she felt toward Eda? Only once in her life had she felt so enamored of a woman and that had been in fifth grade. Her teacher for that year, Mrs. Collins, had been a tall, lovely redhead with an engaging smile and manner. Kaylen had spent the entire school year watching Mrs. Collins with sighs and discreet whimpers, learning the material presented just so she could win one of those charming grins of approval. Later she reasoned that the infatuation with Mrs. Collins had come right when her father had escalated his sexual abuse and this particular teacher had been exceptionally nice, providing a safe haven in the midst of her familial storm.

Had there been other occasions of female attraction? She couldn't remember specifics. Vaguely she remembered short infatuations, crushes on female classmates that lasted weeks at the most. There was something else too, a troubling issue, but her mind wouldn't go there.

Could the problems with her father have made her a...she hesitated even to think the word in connection with herself...a lesbian? But how could that be? She had been married to Chuck for twenty years.

Dismayed by the spiral her mind was taking, Kaylen slipped out of the long T-shirt she'd been lounging in all morning and pulled on a pair of sweatpants and her Tweety Bird T-shirt. After donning a favorite pair of Reeboks she tucked her house keys into her back pocket and left the house.

The spring day was in full flower with sunshine weighing hot on her shoulders. A breeze from the northeast kept things bearable and after stretching out, Kaylen set off at a nice clip. She had always felt her body was too gawky for jogging but race walking was an old passion.

It had kept her sane during those awful years with Chuck, especially when he was at home during the day, enabling her to still have time to herself, time that was hers and hers alone. Had the years with Chuck been so bad? Somewhere buried inside was the knowledge that she had been deeply unhappy for the majority of her life.

Slowly, carefully, she dredged up this knowledge and examined it.

The years with her father had been a nightmare and she had promptly pushed the memory of them away and buried all her emotions, and not only the ones dealing with anger toward her father. Killing these emotions had made her cold, frigid to life, but it had been necessary for her survival. Besides, she wasn't even sure she had ever learned how to express emotion correctly.

She laughed nervously to cover a growing unease and began to breathe very fast as she turned off the shoulder of Route 24 and onto the asphalt road of a quiet residential neighborhood. Fresh greenery surrounded her on all sides and the occasional squirrel scampered nearby. Children, daughters and sons of the homeschooler who lived in the old Marion place, played dodgeball in a wooded yard to Kaylen's right.

Children. They would have saved her, Kaylen thought angrily. If she had only been allowed to bear one child, she might have learned how to love again, love unconditionally and love well.

She had never been able to conceive, whether her fault or Chuck's she never found out. They had just accepted early on that they were not meant to be parents. Chuck, older than she by almost ten years, had refused to go for fertility tests and treatment, even though there was a clinic only forty-five miles away. He said it was God's decision and if He didn't see fit to give them children, then that was the way it was supposed to unfold.

Kaylen, when in a mean mood, often thought Chuck didn't want to try and remedy the problem because he wanted to remain the baby, was afraid that his position as the center of Kaylen's universe would be usurped by a bald, screaming newcomer.

And he had certainly been the center of his wife's world. She had cooked for him, tended his wounds from fishing, hunting and his job at the furniture factory, taken care of paying the bills and saving money, even deciding where they should live and arranging the mortgage. But although she had handled all these day-to-day details, she never really wielded the power in the relationship. What Chuck said was law, and so Kaylen had drifted along behind him, taking care of whatever came up because he expected it of her, not necessarily because she wanted to do it.

But had she ever been happy? Content, maybe? No. More apathetic than anything else.

Anger welled in Kaylen as she puffed her way along White Street, her feet and arms churning rapidly. It had been almost as if she hadn't had a mind of her own.

Though she liked to read in the evenings, Chuck said he didn't want her sitting around with her nose in a book, so she had begun watching television alongside him most nights.

He wasn't a vegetarian, so she had cooked endless meat-based meals, even though the sight of raw meat made her gag.

And sexually? Sexually, she hadn't cared. Chuck had certainly never gone out of his way to please her but then she expected no pleasure. Sex was a painful, demeaning thing forced upon women as part of their wifely "duty." And in her case her daughterly duty as well.

She slowed her frantic pace to a lurching walk. Tears sprouted warmth in her eyes and gushed in two small streams. Gasping, her chest afire with long-buried pain and regret wrapped around a rapidly beating heart, she could walk no more and fell face forward to a grassy bank alongside the road. Turning, she sat tailor-style and covered her face with shaking hands.

How could she have lived forty years in a blind, unfeeling fog? Here she was, in the middle of her life, and she had yet to live. What was fair about that?

She thought of all the people who had passed through her life and realized she had truly loved none of them—not her father, her brothers, or her husband. She had been fond of Peaches, a cat who'd passed away just before Chuck died. And then there had been Melody, her roommate in college. They had been good, close friends until Melody had married a country-western singer and been killed in a plane crash while on tour with him. And now there was only Jane Anne, whom she had learned to care for.

She rubbed at her wet, reddening eyes and used the bottom of her T-shirt to wipe her streaming nose. She watched in emotional pain as the people of this quiet neighborhood went about their business, old men mowing lawns, white-haired ladies tending their gardens, and a teen working on a rusted car.

She thought of Eda with her bright spirit and gentle but energetic ways. Was Eda the person she could finally love? Kaylen nodded with resignation. Yes, this person she could love, simply because she seemed to have no control over it. She, who had always remained in control and shielded from her own emotions, was now thrown headfirst into a total uncontrolled situation where her emotions could and would run riot. Oh yes, she could see it happening.

She sighed. Yes, and she could also see the end of life as she knew it; a life safe, ordered and secure.

If only Eda were a man, she might have been able to salvage something. People would talk, a scandal would develop, but it would pass. After all, it was normal to have a relationship with a man. Even if it was a sordid, short-lived affair or even a long-term affair with a younger man, it would be accepted and only brought up as an occasional chuckle for "remember when" times.

But to fall in love with a woman… Well, it was like her name, not understood and not accepted, ever. She would always be branded "that lesbian woman" and talked about in hushed tones, even long after the novelty had died.

Done with crying, emotions acknowledged and spent, Kaylen mopped at her face with her shirt and rose to walk slowly toward home.

She faced a hell of a choice. She could ignore her burgeoning feelings for Eda and live the rest of her life in an emotional void, regretting love lost and continuing with her sterile meals and movies with Jane Anne. Or she could welcome the possibility of love with open arms, drawing Eda ever closer and saying to hell with everyone who currently populated her life.

Some choice.

CHAPTER TWENTY

"Come on, baby gurrl. Make daddy feel nice."

The words reverberate in her head and Kaylen turns, impatiently jerking loose the sheets, to wrap her form, mummy-like, into a white shroud.

"Get on outta there, you dumb bitch! I shore wish yore ma was here to keep an eye on you. Maybe she'da kept you from gettin' inta such foolishness. I swear, girls ain't nothin' but dumb, just igno'rant. Ya gotta tell 'em where to piss, even."

A laugh echoes. A hand looms large and sudden pain wells, making her eyes feel bounced in her head. A throbbing headache splits the space above her nose.

"Hyram, Jame, can't ya'll watch out for yore sister? She's done got

in the barn and got cow shit all over her."

Other hands grab at her. She is pressed against rough, sweat-and urine-stinking clothes.

"What are you gonna do with her?" It's a boy's whisper, hoarse and curious.

"I dunno," says the older boy. "I'd like to take her out and shoot her though. God, she causes trouble."

She kicks out and feels an intense sensation of pleasure as the kick connects against cloth-covered skin with square power. The pleasure is soon replaced by humiliation, however, as she is dumped into the slimy, frigid water of the horse trough. Boyish braying parts the night.

"Look at her! Ain't no princess now."

But I am a princess, her mind screams.

There is a cherished photograph of her mother and it is kept beneath the straw-stuffed mattress that is her bed. She keeps the tinted print wrapped in an old scarf that was her mother's. The scarf, even after seven years, bears faint traces of her mother's perfume.

She knows where he is sitting. He is in the living room, sitting in the dark, alone. He will be drinking whiskey, whiskey made by his own hands so it is harsh and practically unpalatable. It seems to help him though, seems to take the angry fear from his eyes.

And when he comes to her later that night...

She stuffs the picture away, because he must not know she took it from the things the women carried from the house.

Kaylen turns in her white shroud, her thumb seeking the slot between her teeth for comfort. Sudden sweat sprouts on her brow and under her arms.

And when he comes to her later that night, she sees, with a gleam of moonlight, that his eyes are calm, almost friendly. So she takes what he offers in her hands, the smell unmistakable, a smell inhaled dozens of times before, and she does as he instructs until the pressure eases and her hands and face are sticky and pungent.

Afterward, as always, he is sleepy and wanders off, stumbling past the doorway to the boys' bedroom to collapse on the sofa.

She lies there on her mattress, watching as the cracks in the ceiling talk to her and give her familiar pictures. She swabs her hands and face on the bed sheets trying to clean them.

Snapped by wind, the door to the tool shed slams in the dark night and she is transported back to when the thin arms of a young girl held her safe and close, the girl's skin dry and almost feverish as if she burned from inner fire.

She whispers into the younger Kaylen's hair, pressing parched lips to her forehead from time to time, as if imparting some of her precious internal combustion, as if Kaylen could take it and make it her own, building defenses and walls for protection.

But the young Kaylen isn't sure how to take it from the older girl, even pressing her parted baby lips to hers doesn't help. The warm tongue carries no ticket to help the heat come over. She revels in this heat, however, pressing their bodies close, mingling sweat, smells, breath. Secrets pass, fears rush back and forth between them.

This is before the touching of the big man. Just six years from the mother's death, there have been only hands bearing stinging pain and anger. The hot girl informs her about the other touch, warns her against it, tells her to run away.

There's nowhere to run, she tells the older girl, her words lisping because her front teeth are loose, ready to make room for bigger teeth.

Run to the church, the older girl tells her. The people of the church will protect her. But later she discovers there is no protection, for her or the thin, burning girl. She is only a child, after all, not a princess whose words are much beloved.

On her straw mattress, she pulls out the picture of her mother, turning it so the moonlight will make the captured figure glow. And there she is, her satin dress bright in the light, her hair and eyes dark. Those eyes, filled with life and vitality, are amused eyes; wise. Angel eyes, the little girl calls them, as she tries to make her own eyes feel that way. But in the one ruptured mirror left by the women, she sees that her eyes, though the same color as those portrayed in the photograph, cannot be filled with that look. No matter how charmingly she tilts her uncombed head, the look will not come.

A thin girl's body, once burning but now so cold, dangles high in a barn. Dressed in ripped and faded bib overalls, she seems underdressed as dust motes dance a dirge in a thick shaft of sunlight. Kaylen sees her from below, hearing doves coo in the loft. She cannot scream.

Kaylen awakens suddenly, the white-sheet shroud pulled so tight by her frantic twisting that she can no longer breathe.

CHAPTER TWENTY-ONE

Kaylen didn't see anyone again until Saturday morning. Two days had passed since the dam of her self-inflicted stoicism had burst, but the pain and agony were still fresh in her mind. Those two days had been spent in contemplation, refusing to answer the phone, the door or attend any of the numerous meetings that normally dotted her life.

Jane Anne came by that Saturday morning, yelling through an open window until Kaylen was forced to let her in. Kaylen regretted the action immediately.

"Why didn't you answer your phone?" Jane Anne berated her. "We thought you were dead. I swear Kaylen if that isn't the most thoughtless thing to do. I hope you feel ashamed of yourself."

Jane Anne was visibly angry, bright blotches of red highlighting each of her cheekbones. She watched Kaylen, arms akimbo, breathing heavily.

Kaylen, who hadn't brushed her hair or seriously bathed in two days, eyed her friend with jaundiced, haggard eyes.

"Oh, I can just hear Ellie now, talking about how I probably up and ran off with the man who delivers milk to Lerner's Grocery," she said dully. "Or maybe I died while doing one of those ridiculous yoga poses. You know what a weird hippie I am."

"Now, Kaylen, you're not being fair. All of us care about you. You're one of our little family." Jane Anne began tidying the living room, neatly stacking the piles of newspapers, junk mail and empty dishes. She switched off the endlessly droning television and carried a stack of bowls, overflowing ashtrays, silverware and plates into the kitchen.

"What family? You guys would crucify me as soon as look at me, and you know it," Kaylen called to her retreating back.

Jane Anne reappeared in the doorway and pushed wispy pieces of her graying hair back from her forehead with damp hands. "Okay, Kaylen, what is it? Are you sick? Mad about something? Tell me what's wrong."

Kaylen leaned forward in her easy chair and scrubbed at her face with both hands. Her hands smelled of grape jelly and, removing them, she looked down at her clothing and realized how unkempt she had allowed herself to become. She had been wearing the same ragged T-shirt and shorts for two days.

She turned toward her friend, mouth working as if it wanted to spew a torrent of words. Instead, she stood and said simply, "I'm a mess. I'm going to take a shower."

Jane Anne watched her with puzzlement twisting her features as Kaylen walked unsteadily toward the bathroom.

She was waiting with a pile of clean clothes when Kaylen, wrapped in a towel, emerged from the bathroom.

Kaylen plopped down on the bed next to Jane Anne, feeling better but still very confused. They sat silently a short while.

"Do you want to tell me what's wrong, honey?" Jane Anne said finally. "Maybe talking about it will help."

Kaylen shook her head, her short hair spattering wet droplets.

"No, this is something I have to work out myself. Basically, I just realized I'd been living my whole life like a dead person and I'm not going to do it anymore."

Jane Anne wrinkled her brow. "This is living? Staying holed up in your filthy lair day after day?"

This elicited a small smile from Kaylen, then an abrupt deluge of soundless tears.

"Oh, hey, God, I'm sorry, sugar. I didn't mean to make you get all..."

"It's okay." Kaylen hurried to reassure her, all the while choking back a soft sob. "It happens a lot these days."

"These days? Oh, then it's the change, that's it!" Relief seemed to sweep through Jane Anne and she relaxed against the bed. "Menopause is an awful time. No wonder you don't want to come out and see anyone."

"No, silly, you know I'm dealing just fine with most of that foolishness. This is something different. A reevaluation of my life, I guess. It's just...well, I've always let people tell me what to do, my father, my brothers, Chuck, Ellie and the rest of society, even you. I've gotta stop it somehow." Another sob shook her.

Jane Anne stood impatiently and laid the clothing evenly on the bed, smoothing the folded edges.

"Let me get this straight. You're pissed off and crying because you've had a lot of people in your life who cared about you?" She threw her hands up in exasperation. "What is it with you?"

"Oh, go to hell," Kaylen muttered, bursting into a fresh storm of weeping.

Jane Anne paced the large bedroom, pausing to finger Kaylen's haphazardly placed possessions strewn across the bureau. As if unable to bear the sobbing of her friend, she moved back to the bed and pulled Kaylen to her feet. Wrapping her own slender arms about her, Jane Anne tucked Kaylen's streaming face into the cup-shaped space where shoulder met neck and rubbed her back, still damp from the shower.

"There, there," she cooed. "I think you just need to sleep for a little while until you feel better."

She reached to pull down blankets she had straightened moments before, and slowly lowered Kaylen into the bed. She lifted her friend's long legs and tucked them under the blanket and gently rolled her so she could rub her back and shoulders with soothing hands. Kaylen reached down and tugged loose the towel she was wrapped in and threw it onto the floor.

Jane Anne paused in her ministrations until Kaylen turned toward her and remarked sarcastically. "Don't worry, we're being proper. I'm thoroughly hidden by the covers."

"Oh, would you stop being so foolish," Jane Anne murmured, resuming her massage. "Here, you go to sleep now."

Hours later, Kaylen woke to a still, darkened house. Jane Anne had gone.

Stretching mightily in the bed, she felt much better than she had before Jane Anne's visit, although her mouth felt pasty from crying so much.

Rising, she padded naked into the bathroom where she relieved her bladder and gave her teeth a quick brush. Feeling chilled, she donned the T-shirt and panties Jane Anne left out for her, then fished a pair of worn sweatpants from her bureau drawer. She rubbed lotion on her arms and face and swept a brush through her hair.

Dusk was settling outside and the peeper frogs had begun their nightly cacophony. Kaylen stood in her kitchen doorway listening for some time, finally moving to fetch a glass of iced tea from the refrigerator. She downed the glass in three gulps.

Stepping out the back door and feeling her toes sweep through the cool wet grass, Kaylen realized she felt better than she had in...well, in her whole life. Finally at peace with herself, her world became much more intense. She studied her new yard through the dimness, appreciating anew the beauty of Eda's design.

Gingerly, due to her bare feet, she stepped onto new white gravel, her fingertips reaching out and barely grazing the tips of the small redbud tree just before she reached the dirt of the

116

vegetable garden.

When had Eda brought the trees and planted them? She vaguely remembered persistent knocking on her door, voices calling her name. She had ignored it all, lost in a depression and self-hatred such as she had never known.

Did she love herself now? Perhaps she could look at her reflection now without cringing. Perhaps she could tolerate, and almost like, this woman called Kaylen. After all, it was not too late. She realized now that she had killed her capability to love simply for protection from an experience no child should have to deal with. And later, it had been easy to allow someone else to live her life while she healed and grew.

But now everything had come full circle. She felt born again, alive in a way she couldn't even remember having been alive before. She felt itchy, raw, but ripe as a purple plum, ready to be plucked and savored, ready to pluck and to savor.

She stepped back onto the cool grass and spun around slowly, arms outstretched, feeling the chill of the evening air as it brushed past her arms, her hands, her face.

And when a truck pulled up out in front, its headlights slicing into the darkness of the backyard, she nodded her head sagely, as if the visit had been expected. This was as it should be.

CHAPTER TWENTY-TWO

"Hey Kaylen, are you all right? I was gettin' pretty worried about you."

Eda was standing on the front porch. Backlit by the harsh outside light, her wispy blond hair surrounded her head in a surrealistic halo.

"Angel of salvation," Kaylen muttered softly.

"What?" Eda's voice quavered with worry.

"I'm sorry. Yes, I'm fine, come in." She stepped back, allowing Eda access. "What are you doing wandering around? Shouldn't you be at home with your family?"

"Well…" Seeming cautious, uncertain, Eda moved along the front foyer into the living room. "I don't live at home anymore. I live in an apartment below my grandparents. They give me cheap rent and I like that a lot."

Kaylen followed Eda into the living room and pulled Eda's light jacket from her shoulders. "So why did you move out?"

Eda shrugged, standing in the middle of the room, eyeing Kaylen with curiosity. "Differences. I prefer my life to be private."

"That's good, good. Sit down. I'll get us some tea. How about hot tea? Mint?"

As if feeling more at ease, Eda sat on the sofa. "Yum, that sounds wonderful."

Kaylen disappeared into the kitchen to put the kettle on.

"It's amazing the rules and regulations southern women put on themselves, isn't it?" Eda asked when Kaylen reappeared a few moments later. She had been leafing through a *Southern Living* magazine Jane Anne had left on the coffee table. "I mean, you have to dress a certain way, even eat a certain way. Here's an article about the proper foods to prepare for a funeral. As if that mattered."

"Oh, but it does," Kaylen reassured her. "I know. I've been living in this mess my whole life. You play by the rules or they won't let you play at all."

Eda eyed Kaylen sideways, a Mona Lisa smile curving her weathered lips. "So who wants to play their games? Couldn't you just develop some games of your own?"

Kaylen laughed from the doorway. "You're so damned smart. Who says I want to play alone? That can get pretty boring." She moved back into the kitchen.

"Here, let me help you," Eda said following her. "Tell the truth now. Isn't it pretty boring doing things the proper, southern way?"

Kaylen paused, a ceramic mug held in one hand. "Pretty boring, yes."

Eda laughed her special tinkling laugh and said, "What can I do to help?"

"Well, you can fetch some cookies from the cookie box and put them on a plate."

"What's a cookie box?"

Kaylen made a tsking sound with her tongue and teeth. "It's that metal monstrosity over beside the refrigerator. I inherited it from my Granny Esther."

Eda approached the large silver box resting on the counter. It was decorated with tarnished carving around the edges. She opened it.

"Hey, what's this bowl of water next to the cookies for?"

Kaylen was busy separating tea bags. "Oh, one thing I can't stand is a hard cookie. The water lets them absorb moisture so they're soft."

Eda reacted with puzzled silence.

"I know it's a little strange," Kaylen said finally, with a short laugh, "but it's just the way I do it. I hope you don't mind them soft."

"No, I like cookies that are soft too." She removed several of the chocolate chip cookies and arranged them neatly about the edges and center of a plate.

They each carried trays into the living room and placed the items side by side on the coffee table. They were very close and Kaylen could smell Eda's sunny, windblown scent. Her hands ached to reach out and pull the tiny woman toward her. She wanted to let her hands roam with abandon across bare skin, wanted to bury her face in the crevice where neck met shoulder.

Kaylen realized she was breathing fast and her heart was thudding in her chest.

Eda reached out then, took one of Kaylen's hands and tucked it within both of hers. "I don't know what has happened over the last few days but I've really missed you," she said in a low voice. "There's something about you, something I feel when I'm around you..."

She sighed, the intake of breath ragged. "I'm sorry. I'm babbling. Just please, please don't shut me out again. I...I need to be with you now."

Kaylen felt perilously close to tears again and she fought valiantly, her face working. It was no use; the tears rose with hot freedom and blazed new trails along her cheeks. Embarrassed, she pulled away and turned her back to Eda.

"Oh, Christ," Eda said softly, "what have I done now?"

"Please, ignore me," Kaylen said, trying to smile through her tears. "I've been an emotional wreck."

She could feel Eda watching her. "Do you want to talk about it?"

Kaylen shook her head, lips pressed together. She bent to pour the tea, effectively closing the discussion.

"Hey, I bought a movie. Would you like to watch it? It's had good reviews. It's in the truck. I'll get it." Eda, her phrases like bullets, patted the pockets of her jeans seeking keys. She grabbed up her jacket that was resting beside the door.

Kaylen nodded and smiled in relief. She desperately needed a distraction before she became a complete fool.

The movie sent her into a new maelstrom of emotion. It was a recent release about a woman who travels to Reno, Nevada for a divorce. While awaiting the finalization of the paperwork, she struggles with romantic feelings she develops for a young lesbian.

As the story unfolded, Kaylen felt a surge of delight overtake trepidation. She lifted the movie cover from the coffee table. *Desert Hearts.* Helen Shaver. Patricia Charbonneau. Her eyes lifted to the television screen and she felt mesmerized by the beauty of the two women as they moved through an intricate dance of seduction. And when they kissed in the rain, she felt warmth suffuse her body. Later, when they pressed together on a hotel room bed, Kaylen's breathing stopped for a long moment.

She felt Eda's gaze on her but fear of what might happen if she met that gaze kept her eyes fixed on the screen until the credits rolled. Only then could she breath normally again.

"I think it was neat the way that Vivian was suddenly empowered, don't you?" Eda asked after switching off the set.

"Umm hmm, it was…something."

Eda took the videotape from the player and slipped it into its cardboard jacket.

"Did you like the movie, Kaylen?" she asked softly, eyes on

the cover and head tilted nonchalantly.

Kaylen felt suddenly warmed again, though still not understanding this new, eggshell-strewn ground on which she walked.

"Yes, Eda," she replied, her tone dulcet. "I did enjoy it, a lot. Thank you."

Eda turned and bestowed one of her brilliant smiles. "I'm glad, Kaylen."

They played cards then and Kaylen made a pot of coffee. Eda told her about a trip into Raleigh to pick up the trees, sharing a hilarious tale about how the second gear in her truck decided to develop a bad case of rheumatism in the middle of downtown traffic, causing her no end of embarrassment and trouble.

They talked about which herbs Kaylen wanted in her side garden and this sent them off into a long informative talk about the various uses of herbs, whether medicinal, culinary, fragrant or cosmetic.

About one in the morning, Eda rose and said she had to head for home. Slowly, and in silence, the two women straightened the kitchen, took the dishes in from the living room and washed them, and Eda even plumped the sofa cushions.

"I really enjoyed myself," she told Kaylen at the door, "and I'm glad everything's okay with you now."

Kaylen nodded, catching her bottom lip with her teeth. "Well, not everything but we'll talk about it sometime."

"Good. You can trust me, you know that, don't you?"

"Of course."

Eda's face brightened. "I know what you need. Some pampering, is all. Is there any way you can come over to my house for dinner tomorrow?"

"I don't know," Kaylen said doubtfully. "It's Sunday. Don't you spend it with your family?"

"I sometimes go to church with them, that's all."

"I have church too," Kaylen added quickly.

"I mean later, though, like for supper. Do you think you can?"

Seeing the eagerness and joy lighting the young face below hers, Kaylen felt hard-pressed to say anything rather than no. "Sure, what time do you want me?"

"About seven, I guess, or whenever you can get there. Listen, I live just off Catholic, on Summerhill Road. Do you know where that is?" At Kaylen's nod she continued. "Just go down it about four blocks and I'm on the left in the basement. The house number is four-three-four. Can you remember that?"

"Yeah, but I'll jot it down. I'm old, you know," Kaylen responded with sarcasm.

Eda laughed, the sound sending a ripple of warmth through Kaylen, and then she drew Kaylen into an embrace.

Later Kaylen would not remember how it happened, just the sensation of being held by the fierce little dynamo—thrilling and somehow hot. The contact lasted for just the right amount of time, not long enough to really say anything, and then Eda was gone, calling "Until tomorrow" into the night air.

Kaylen closed the door, grinding her teeth and cursing this stupid social ambiguity that resulted from such strong taboos and mores. Why couldn't each of them just say and act how they really felt. Then a paroxysm of fear stabbed her. Suppose Eda didn't desire her?

Swamped with doubt, Kaylen sought her bed and relief from a whirling mind.

CHAPTER TWENTY-THREE

Kaylen rose before the sun and, wearing only a thin robe, walked outside to her vegetable garden. Feeling a trifle foolish, but determined, she let the robe slip from her shoulders and pool on the ground. She lay down then, with fragile nakedness, on the cool, tilled earth between the rows of carrot tops and snap bean vines.

Not exactly sure why she had the urge to lie unclothed in the soft, loamy dirt, she nevertheless went with the feeling and enjoyed the experience fully, lying there for well over half an hour as the world woke up around her.

It surprised her how early the birds began to sing, long before the sun even peeped over the mountain. And how incredibly wet dew felt. When she stretched out her arms and grasped the supple yet strong stems of the garden plants on either side, she released a cool torrent upon her skin, the droplets very fat and very cold.

There was a strange juxtaposition of sensation that assaulted her as well. The earth was rough-soft under her body and she felt a sinking, a settling as one with it. The feeling brought to mind biblical terminology; ashes to ashes, dust to dust, and the fact of knowing, of becoming one.

At the same time she felt light, as if she were part of the sky, yet not of the sky. She imagined seeing her physical essence lying there in the garden, body thin as a rail, breasts spare and sagging, her belly wrinkled and soft, pubic hair mangled and beginning to lose its definition as a triangle of darkness. Laughter spewed from her then and she was pulled forcefully back to earth, grounded hard, yet still free, liberated. And though liberated, she knew her limits and realized she was not yet ready to be caught lolling naked in her garden, especially by her neighbors and the morning commuters on Route 24.

So, as day gently kissed the morning sky to wakefulness, she scurried into the house, small clods of soil pattering to the ground behind her.

The sound was very much like rain.

CHAPTER TWENTY-FOUR

Throughout the day, going to Eda's for dinner grew to be an event of great magnitude in Kaylen's life. Many times she paused, hand on the telephone, ready to call and tell her she couldn't make it. She realized finally that the gesture was moot anyway; she didn't have Eda's home number, only the Helios business number.

Church was out of the question; she would have never been able to sit still during one of Reverend Johnson's long-winded sermons. So she had called Jane Anne early and pleaded off, using her mysterious emotional instability and a desire for solitude as an excuse.

Left alone though, doubts taunted her. What would a lovely young girl want with an old woman?

Kaylen walked to the large ornate mirror in her seldom-used

dining room and studied her reflection. A gaunt, aging woman stared back at her. There were a few fine wrinkles around the tired brown eyes, noticeable even when she wasn't smiling. Laugh lines creased her good-sized mouth and even her teeth became more discolored each year, seeming to grow larger and more frightening as the gums receded.

Why did people call the wrinkles around the mouth laugh lines? Did it mean they came from laughing a lot or because people often laughed at them on another person?

It was ridiculous. She could be Eda's mother. There was a fifteen-year gulf between them that no amount of pretense or deliberate ignorance could do away with. Wearily, Kaylen mussed her thick mop of graying hair. Who was she fooling — besides herself? Even though she often felt fifteen on the inside she was a full forty on the outside.

And the thought that Eda wanted only her friendship filled her with dismay. How could she be a friend to Eda when she wanted to touch her every time they were together?

She eyed her reflection ruefully once more and then flopped onto the sofa. So, was she destined to live out the rest of her days a lonely, frustrated lesbian who not only never was allowed to come out of the closet but also never even got to practice her newfound queerness, not even once?

Perhaps they *could* be friends. Eda was delightful to be with and Kaylen felt so comfortable talking with her. She would just have to be strong—if Eda desired only friendship—and do her best to maintain a discreet distance between their bodies.

Their bodies. Her mind conjured an image of Eda, reclining half-naked in the artist's studio. Then the image changed. Eda was naked, except for delightful bands of green, inherent to her alienness.

She was a creature of greenery and of the sun, playing like a frolicking faun in the dappled forest sunlight.

Kaylen, walking serenely through the deep forest, spies her one day and afterward is drawn back to the same clearing again and again to watch the forest sprite child dance merrily in the glade, her toe tips seeming to float above the ground as she spins and whirls.

Occasionally fairies joined her, bright spots of color that seemed to clothe her in a dust storm of lights. Brownies came to watch, their rich sepia coats vibrating in the wind of her passage. The sprite handled the gnomes well, giving back their ribald sexual innuendoes as good as she got. She, though tempting them, always managed to slither from their possessive grasp at the last minute, leaving puzzled amusement on their heavily bearded faces.

One day, while tending to the needs of a wounded bird, the sprite spies Kaylen and knows, with an eerie forest canniness, that the woman has been watching and longing for her for some time. With a flash she is at Kaylen's side, urging her to dance. Before Kaylen knows what is happening, she is caught up in the dance, bending and pirouetting in steps that have suddenly become her knowledge. Her clothing falls from her in a tattered stream and warmth washes over her.

She realizes why the sprite dances. The feeling bursts in a kaleidoscope of colors and loud gasps flee Kaylen's lips. Never has she experienced such ecstasy. And she dances on, the sprite at her side, until exhaustion overtakes them and they fall to the ground, a heaving, panting heap of quivering flesh.

The sprite, who has Eda's face banded by stripes of green, eyes Kaylen with a merry and knowing sidelong glance. She kisses Kaylen with heated lips and they celebrate a marriage of sorts, fairies as attendants and all the forest creatures as witness. Music sounds throughout the forest and Kaylen has forgotten her past.

Kaylen had dozed off while frolicking with the sprite and when next she woke, saw it was close to five o'clock. Jolted immediately awake by the lateness of the hour, she rushed to get ready for Eda.

First there was a long, hot bath, using a rare lavender soap she had received as a gift once and had been saving. The rising vapor of sharp scent relaxed her and her mind played out various sexual and innocent scenarios at Eda's house. Arising in a cloud of fragrance, erotically charged, she patted dry and moved into the bedroom.

Seated at her vanity table, Kaylen dug through drawers until she found the usual paint for erotic interludes, eye shadow, face powder, mascara and lipstick. She laid the items in a row on the vanity table and looked in the lighted mirror. Her eyes fastened on every flaw and she mentally reviewed how she could improve or conceal each imperfection. She smiled. Opening one of the drawers, she defiantly swept all the cosmetics into it and shut it firmly. This was a new life. She would go to Eda as she was, old, but honest. She flipped off the vanity light and rose to dress.

She agonized over a bra for some time but, in keeping with honesty, threw it against the far wall. Wearing nothing but her best satin panties, she flipped through her closet seeking the right garment for this special evening. Knowing she wanted to wear a dress, it just felt right somehow, she pushed aside all the floral monstrosities women her age were supposed to wear. She was almost in a panic, afraid she had nothing appropriate, when her eyes lit on a dress she had fallen in love with long ago.

After unzipping its stiff plastic sleeve, inhaling joyfully the scent of the citrus pomander she had stored with it, she lifted out the dress. Holding it in front of her body and looking in a full-length mirror, she deeply regretted the fact she had never worn it before, while she was still young and pretty. Oh, she had wanted to, numerous times, but Chuck had deemed it too revealing and it had remained stored away, a buried fantasy.

Slowly she spread the dress on the bed and found a low-cut satin chemise in her top bureau drawer. The feel of the satin as it slid across her newly awakened skin made her gasp and then laugh at her foolishness. Finally the dress. She lifted it and slid its watered silk sleekness along her arms and down her body. Her eyes closed as she enjoyed the thrill of donning the fragrant, cool garment. She adjusted the fit, her eyes still closed, then turned toward the mirror, and opened her eyes.

It was perfect. She was almost beautiful again. The color was somewhere between a red and a purple, almost a plum, but really indefinable. The quality of the silk caused the color to shimmer as she moved so naming a color didn't matter. The style was flattering, with soft folds of silk crossing low on her chest almost to the waist. The skirt hugged her hips and dropped to just below the knee. She wished for a fleeting moment that the garment weren't sleeveless—her arms were spotty and leaning toward flabby—but decided it was still the perfect dress.

She chose against stockings and merely slipped soft skimmers of black leather onto her feet. There was little she could do with her hair, other than brush it so little wispy curls frolicked around the nape of her neck. After dabbing a rich woodsy scent on her pulse points, woodsy to honor her latest Eda fantasy, she was ready.

As it was still just before six, she forced her mind to relax and she slowly enjoyed a cigarette.

There was no way to know what to expect, she told her galloping mind and hopeful heart. Still, she thought of the quiet way Eda had asked about the movie and other subtle possibilities that said the young woman was just as smitten as she was. Could she be that fortunate? Could she still find love twenty years after she was supposed to? Or would the evening with Eda be just as sterile as her time with Jane Anne? Only the evening would tell, and as yet, it was keeping its secrets.

CHAPTER TWENTY-FIVE

"Yes, Mama, I'm fine. Really," Jane Anne protested into the telephone. "I don't know why you worry so about me. I can take care of myself."

"I bet you're not even touching those vitamins I sent you," Tansy Viar told her daughter, her tone peevish. "I don't know why I waste my money on you."

"Mama, really, I've been taking the vitamins. They taste bad but I take one every day. Honest." Jane Anne rolled her eyes as she moved to the refrigerator and opened the door.

"Good. Mind that you do. Doctor Rollins assured me they're the best on the market and they don't come cheap. You probably couldn't even afford them on that piddling salary they pay you up there. I don't know why you don't come back home and work at the public library here. I saw just last week where they need people."

"Probably aides, Mama. That pays less than this job."

Jane Anne pulled mustard, cheese and lettuce from the refrigerator and balanced all three items along with the phone as she made her way to the kitchen table. Placing the items carefully on the table, she moved to the breadbox.

"Well, you remember Kelly James? She's working there now, not that she needs to, mind, that husband of hers has made a fortune in the contracting business. He does all the houses in the area here and she wears three huge diamonds besides her wedding band."

"Oh shit," Jane Anne whispered as she licked mustard from her index finger.

"What's that, honey? You say something?" Tansy queried.

"I said, 'she does?' Just imagine that."

"Yes, it's amazing to be around her, those diamonds are so bright. We had our annual historic house tour just last week and I thought those diamonds were going to blind every last body on the bus. No one said anything though, that just isn't done, but we all noticed, I can tell you that. I don't know why your father won't buy me another ring. Lord knows, he can afford it now that the Peterson contract came through."

"Mama, you already have four diamonds yourself. Isn't that enough?" Jane Anne took a small bite of her sandwich and reached under the kitchen counter for the bottle of sweet soda she had splurged on at the Food Lion in Freshwater last week.

"I just don't like the settings on two of those, you know that. Your father has no taste when it comes to picking diamonds. I can't believe I let him loose in a jewelry store. I should make a point to go with him but then that just isn't done, now is it? Shame."

Tansy paused for breath. "Jane Anne Viar, are you eating?" she screeched suddenly. "I've told you a hundred times if I've told you once, you don't eat or drink while talking on the telephone. Where are your manners, girl? Just because I'm your mama doesn't mean you can be rude and selfish to me!"

Jane Anne immediately dropped the sandwich onto the tabletop where it twisted into an intriguing S-shape, spilling cheese, mustard and lettuce in a sluggish flow. She swallowed quickly.

"I'm sorry, Mama, I just forgot. I haven't had a thing since lunch. I wasn't paying attention," Jane Anne said slowly.

Tansy made a harsh disapproving sound. "Well, that's always been your problem. You just don't pay attention. What about that Carlin boy, loved you like the sun rose and set in your face. You didn't pay him a bit of mind and he must have chased you for the better part of two years. You could have married him. You know what he's doing now? He's a lawyer. See what you lose when you don't pay attention, young lady?"

Jane Anne felt anger stir in her gut. Wouldn't this blasted woman ever shut up and leave her alone? Tansy's voice droned on and Jane Anne let her mind wander, a dangerous, reckless occupation when her mother was talking. Still, she wanted to hurt the woman somehow. When the next lull came in Tansy's tirade, Jane Anne cleared her throat.

"Any word from Martin, Mama? Has anyone found him yet?" Tansy's sudden indrawn breath gave Jane Anne a world of satisfaction.

"No, not a peep, and you know it just breaks my heart. Why would my baby boy just run off like that without a word to anyone in all these many years? I just know he's lying dead down in that jungle somewhere, bit by some jungle snake or something." Tears choked her voice and Jane Anne could picture her mother swiping at her dry eyes with a lace handkerchief.

"I just can't talk about it," she said at last, effectively closing the subject. "I want to talk about you, the sweet baby I still have."

"I've told you, Mama, I'm doing just fine." Jane Anne sighed, eyeing her sandwich with longing.

"So, tell me, is there a man in your life yet?" Tansy's voice rang with eagerness.

Hating the answer she must give, but knowing better than to lie—mainly because her mama would be on the next plane out of Atlanta just to meet the man her daughter named—Jane Anne answered dully. "No, Mama, Mister Right hasn't come along yet."

"Mister Right, hmmph!" Tansy responded. "You just push the men away, Janey. I don't understand why you do that. You need to settle down and give me some grandchildren. Lord knows, you're the only one who can give me grandchildren and here you are letting all your good childbearing years just slip away. I swear, I don't know what gets in your head. You need to pretty yourself up some. I've taught you so much about bettering yourself but you just seem to ignore everything I say..."

Jane Anne had had enough. "Mama, I've got to go," she said suddenly. "My friend Kaylen is knocking on the door."

"But we...we're not done talking," Tansy protested.

"I can't send her away, Mama," Jane Anne whispered urgently. "That wouldn't be right."

"Well, that's true. You tell her your mama said hi now, and don't you forget to write me this month. Your last letter was mighty short, and please, work on your penmanship, honey, it's simply getting atrocious."

"Okay, Mama, I will. 'Bye, love you." She hung up quickly before Tansy had a chance to respond.

Jane Anne backed away from the telephone as if it had suddenly grown fangs and growled. Whirling, she set her gaze out the kitchen window, her eyes unfocused and unseeing. Her fingers shook as she raised them to her face and rubbed her cheekbones with angry roughness. Slim fingers crept up and began to tug at her hair, enjoying the pain in her scalp. The knot at the back of her head loosened and her hair fell to swirl about her shoulders.

Some time later she realized she had pulled out several swatches of hair, her head hurt, and her mouth was bleeding inside where she had bitten it. Alarmed, she raced into the bathroom and checked the mirror to make sure no visible damage showed which she would have to explain. Ignoring the haggardness of her face, she was satisfied that no sign of her growing insanity could be seen.

CHAPTER TWENTY-SIX

The yard at Eda's grandparents' house was a testament to her landscaping skill and to the length of time she had been practicing her art. Well-established shrubs—green yew and juniper, lavender lilac, pink azaleas, golden forsythia and even a well-pruned bank of creamy honeysuckle—bordered and decorated the front yard.

Flower beds were scattered in an eye-pleasing plan. Kaylen saw zinnias, peonies, tulips, pansies, and in a sunny, less-shaded place, a riot of early petunias. Blooming redbud and dogwood trees added graceful bursts of color at higher levels.

Pulling into the tree-shaded driveway, Kaylen followed asphalt that ran alongside the house then looped around and down. The drive ended at a small parking area and she pulled her car in next to Eda's small green pickup truck.

Eda had been at work in the back as well but in a different

manner. Taking advantage of a nearby creek, she had crafted an elaborate yet somehow simple Japanese rock garden. Huge boulders had been uncovered along the creek bank and others added to create a descending display. Exotic plants had been placed amid the rocks adding visual interest and vivid color. Willow trees and flowering cherries finished off the rounded, dome-shaped scheme.

Approaching Eda's door, Kaylen breathed in the fragrance of mock orange and purple lilac, trying to calm down. She didn't quite understand why she was so nervous; someone who liked flowers and beauty as much as Eda did had to be a wonderful human being and no threat. But the thought of what hell her life would become if her friends discovered her feelings for this petite woman made an evening with Eda seem not so harmless.

There was enough delay after Kaylen rang the doorbell for her to wonder whether Eda was indeed home. But soon she was there, with a wide smile and the much relieved Kaylen was drawn into a brief embrace.

"Oh, gosh, look at you," Eda said, eyes roving across her in appreciation.

Eda, too, had taken great pains with her appearance. Her long hair was down, the last few inches caught in a strip of fabric behind her back. Her face looked freshly scrubbed and she was wearing a simple satin chemise shirt in a rich forest green color. The hue of the tunic-length garment deepened the color of her eyes while making them luminescent at the same time. The jeans she wore were of a deep indigo blue. Kaylen had to force her eyes to look away or she would have remained on the front walk forever, drinking in the beauty of the young woman.

"You look great," Kaylen managed.

Eda laughed and pulled Kaylen inside.

The smell of good cooking assailed her as she entered the small terrace apartment and she commented on it.

"I love to cook," admitted Eda, "but seldom get the chance. It's always a treat for me."

They watched each other in awkward silence a moment, then

Eda smiled and said, "I'm so glad you're here. Look, why don't you wander around and make yourself at home. I'll check the food."

She disappeared into the kitchen and Kaylen was left in the spacious living room which was furnished in a southwestern style, with low, comfortable furniture and sand and pastel prints on the walls. The thick scatter rugs and various implements hanging in clusters about the room bore a definite Native American influence. Dried strawflowers filled a large buff pottery urn situated in the far corner.

Kaylen wandered down a wide hallway and passed the door to a bedroom, probably Eda's. The room, however, was not furnished as one would expect from a typical twenty-five-year-old woman. There was none of the usual lacy frippery, useless pillows or stuffed animals. Instead books were stacked neatly in every available space, on the bureau, the floor and, though the large bed that dominated the room was cleared and neatly made, it seemed as if they were usually on the bed as well. The hardwood floors were covered with thick beige rugs, the windows with flowing beige drapes, and the bedspread was a startling but beautifully rich purple color.

Coming back along the hall toward the living room, Kaylen passed what she had first assumed was a second bedroom. Peering in, she saw the room was practically empty save for a small altar placed against the back wall and a few easy chairs. Several carved icons stood to either side of the low altar, which had been fashioned from a large slab of dark, polished wood. Drawn irresistibly into the room, she saw that the icons, too, were of wood, some light-hued, some dark, many done in a bas-relief style. Most depicted faces, faces of merry-eyed, laughing women, or strong, frowning women. There were two carvings of men, both bearing strange stag-like horns on their heads. An unusual odor wafted up to Kaylen's nostrils, a bit like incense, a bit like candle wax, and a secondary note, a type of fragrant oil or spice.

"Neat room, huh?" Eda said, coming up behind her like

smoke on a gentle wind.

Kaylen pulled her eyes from the strange objects scattered across the altar and met Eda's gaze with an apologetic look. "I'm sorry, I shouldn't have intruded."

Eda took Kaylen's arm and led her from the room. "What intrusion? I asked you into my home, didn't I? That shows how much I trust you, and like you, and that I could share my personal side with you."

"The carvings are quite lovely," Kaylen said as they neared the small kitchen. "What do they represent?"

Eda eyed her new friend with mischievous delight. "Oh, please, don't get me started on that, we'll talk of nothing else all night. Let's eat, okay? Then we'll explore my strange beliefs."

"Okay. Anyway, I'm starving," Kaylen agreed.

A small table had been set with clear crystal plates and goblets and a preponderance of creamy white gardenias and magnolia blooms in the center. The scent was rich and heady.

"Oh, my goodness," Kaylen exclaimed. "Wherever did you get blooms this early?" She rushed to the table and cupped her hands around one of the bowl-sized flowers and inhaled the fragrance.

Eda watched Kaylen like a proud, doting parent. "I have lots of friends with greenhouses, remember?"

She filled their wineglasses, gestured for Kaylen to sit, even holding her chair, then disappeared into the kitchen.

Kaylen sipped the ice cold wine and was amazed when it flowed along her throat like nectar. "Holy shit," she whispered.

"What?" asked Eda, coming up behind her with a large ceramic serving tray.

"What is this heavenly concoction," she asked, studying the pale golden wine in her glass.

Eda chuckled as she sat a steaming plate of pasta at each place setting.

"It's a family recipe my brother brought from Germany. I won't tell you all the ingredients but one is honey and another is wine. If I said any more, someone would tie me to a tree and give me fifty lashes."

She disappeared again and Kaylen took another sip of the delightful wine as Eda came back, this time carrying a green vegetable mixture, lightly steamed, and a basket of fresh, fragrant rolls.

"Go easy on that wine," she told Kaylen with amusement as she took her seat. "It has quite a kick because it goes down so smooth."

Kaylen quickly set the glass aside and gave her attention to the feast before her. But she kept coming back to the wine like a bewitched lover.

They talked of mundane things, local happenings, the work on Kaylen's yard, and the surprising growth of their sleepy little town. Then Kaylen, feeling warm and carefree from the wine and good food, asked about the altar. What did religion mean for Eda?

Eda took the tipsy Kaylen by the hand and led her back to the quiet room. Imitating Eda's lead and slipping her shoes from her feet, Kaylen followed her inside.

Kaylen felt a strange power vibrating in the room this time, quiet, still, waiting, but with subtle movement, subtle life.

Eda had brought one of the perfumed gardenia blossoms from the table and she knelt and placed it in the middle of the altar. Taking up a stick match, she swiped it against the wall and lit the candles on the altar, three candles in the back, one green and one red, the middle one white. Other white candles were placed at various points on and about the altar. These too she lit, all the while mumbling something just under her breath.

Kaylen, kneeling beside her, wanted very badly to ask what she was saying but could only watch in a peaceful entrancement as Eda went through a familiar ritual. Finally words became audible.

"Holy Mother, Green of Earth, we come before you now in celebration of fresh love and innocence."

Kaylen tore her eyes from the flaming, glistening altar and fastened them on Eda, who was sprinkling something onto a little black disc. Immediately sweet smoke erupted, clouding the air around them.

Eda seemed to glow mistily in the candlelight and smoke and Kaylen felt a sense of emptiness wash through her being. To have a faith such as this, a place to go for sustenance and rebirth, away from the staid pews filled with judgmental folk, was a blessing.

Eda talked on softly, speaking an old language that was English but yet was too beautiful to be what she spoke each day. Kaylen heard verses, then long bouts of prose, and poetry again, with Eda sometimes being supplicant and other times wearing the guise of the Goddess. She finally turned to Kaylen, in human or Goddess form Kaylen wasn't sure, and lifted a heavy, beaded necklace from the altar. She passed it through the candle flame, smoke from the incense, and through water in which she had dissolved some fine white powder. Bearing it in her tiny hands, she lifted it above Kaylen and placed it over her head, dropping its gentle weight onto her neck.

Perhaps it was imagination, but Kaylen suddenly felt suffused with new life. Years faded away as she fingered the dark copper and wood beads. A spicy aroma met her nose then and she saw Eda palming a thick, clear oil in her hands. She warmed the oil for a moment, then, with shining eyes, anointed Kaylen's hands, her arms, and finally her face and neck with the heady mixture.

In her inebriated condition, the feel of Eda's hands finally touching her bare flesh proved almost too much for Kaylen to bear. Her eyes closed and she shivered at the incredible sensation. Though Eda's hands were callused from hard work, they were soft and fluent on her skin as a man's could never be. It was the touch of a mother, a sister, but so erotic Kaylen's mind began to burn.

A small sigh escaped Eda and Kaylen opened her eyes. She immediately saw the desire flaming in Eda's eyes and she knew, without a doubt, what would happen.

The soft voice seems to come from far away.
"This is the way of my religion," the voice whispers to Kaylen. It was just beside, then behind, then coming from the very walls themselves.

"It's love, only love, the indisputable power of that love. And love is manifested in nature, the bounty of the Mother Earth."

"Yes, I've felt that," Kaylen whispers urgently as shadows rustle at her sides.

"What is the one force that will always prevail over all humankind?"

The question rebounds with a sibilant hiss. Kaylen knows and her core glows warm because she knows. "It's nature. Nature can always best humans."

"And nature is?"

"Us, you and me. Nature is us." Her smile is victorious as she draws her knees to her chest and embraces them with her clasped arms.

Eda appeared and her eyes frolicked with Kaylen's. She raised one fragrant palm and smoothed it along the older woman's face then pressed her parted lips to Kaylen's.

"How old are you, really?" Kaylen asked when the intoxicating kiss ended. She dropped her chin, embarrassed to have asked, but Eda's fingers raised that chin to resume eye contact.

"Age doesn't live here. Women are ageless and eternal because we make it so. Kiss me again, I'm on fire."

These words lent ignition to Kaylen's own desire and suddenly she changed from caterpillar to butterfly, from planet to glowing star.

Leaping, shivering waves touched her body, followed by the hot presence of breath and moist lips. A body moved toward her from the window-lit darkness, kneeling on the bed and wrapping small, strong hands across her swelling, peaking breasts. Heat and coolness battled across her bare skin, skin that was clothed with mottled shadows in the moonlight.

Moist lips whispered against hers and a demanding tongue teased her until she moved against the form with harsh longing.

A firm appendage of that warm, hard body somehow insinuated itself and spread her legs. A moment of old, ingrained fear gave her pause but nature ruled and she opened, welcoming the rounded, muscular leg that was thrust between her own.

142

She felt her body moving in an ancient half-forgotten rhythm and small bursts of ecstasy multiplied somewhere deep within. A form suckled her breast and the pleasure grew until her hands reached blindly and found other firm globes of flesh topped by small rigid peaks. Continuing to explore, she discovered wide, smooth expanses of flower-petal skin and finally a heated crevice filled with sea foam.

Moans sounded against her chest and her nipple was suddenly freed, the coolness of air as enticing as the lips had been. These lips found her mouth for heart-stopping moments then roamed across her body, occasionally stopping to graze. Caught in a maelstrom of sensation, Kaylen could only allow her head to fall back as small bubbles of sound escaped her mouth.

She saw she was underwater then, powerful currents of warm water gushing between her legs and under her arms. Leaning forward, she sought and found soft, sweet-tasting skin to kiss and caress with fierce fingers. But when the strong thigh moved as if to leave its home between hers, she whimpered in hurt and abandonment and drew the body closer, pressing her own thigh to the newborn kitten hovering just above.

More kisses then and Kaylen dropped into the being that was Eda. The kisses drew her away from her earthbound self and she was again that super-being that flew above the town of Freshwater, a hero to all.

Eda's hands were on her, moving against her tirelessly. It began to happen then, so suddenly and unexpectedly that Kaylen was frightened. How dare this happen with another person present, when she was not alone, and especially not by her own hand? But as she wailed out her pleasure, she saw she would never be alone again, no matter whether this body-shattering event, this *petite morte* of the French, happened with the help of another or by her own hand.

Several pieces of a life puzzle finally clicked into place and she happily passed through the initiation into a new womanhood. Kaylen joined her sisters from the beginning of time, sisters who, though contentedly serving as wives and mothers, know the secret of where true pleasure is hidden.

Some time later her hand stole up to heft the weight of the copper and wood necklace and she realized this was not a dream, not one of her many rich fantasies. Eda held her, one small hand resting in the center of Kaylen's belly as if protecting that power center of pleasure she had so recently awakened. Her hair, fragrant and delightful, brushed Kaylen's mouth.

Feeling Kaylen's movement, she lifted her head and sought her eyes. Kaylen smiled and moved onto her side so she could face the younger woman.

Eda pressed warm lips to the end of Kaylen's nose.

Words could never convey their thoughts at that moment so they communicated with their eyes, their slender, white bodies lit by the rays of a bright moon, the only witness to their intimacy.

Night noises intruded faintly through the open windows of Eda's bedroom—a passing car, a television program in the distance, teens calling to one another, and below it all, the sound of water rushing across rocks and moss.

Kaylen drew the tip of one finger along the cleft between Eda's breasts. "You didn't..."

"Not yet, but the night is still young."

Kaylen grinned eagerly and pressed her mouth to the slope of Eda's shoulder.

"Let me help," she whispered hoarsely, delicious passion choking her. "Tell me what you like."

CHAPTER TWENTY-SEVEN

What could have been an awkward breakfast the next morning was filled instead with loving glances and brief caresses bestowed in passing. The first half hour after rising was spent clearing the remains from the previous night's dinner. This the two women accomplished in almost complete silence.

Later sitting at the table opposite one another, steaming cups of coffee before them, they smiled and broke the comfortable quiet.

"Do you feel..." Eda began, ducking her blond head as if afraid of the answer.

"No," Kaylen replied hurriedly. "I feel as though last night was the greatest thing to ever happen to me."

Eda took Kaylen's hand and caressed it softly, her gaze fond.

"How about you?" Kaylen returned softly. "Was..."

Eda, seeing that Kaylen held a cigarette in her other hand, sat back and offered a light. "I feel a lot better than yesterday. I knew I had to make love with you and I was so afraid you'd reject me or even hate me afterward."

Kaylen leaned in for the light. She was astonished by Eda's comment. "I told you before, I could never hate you, Eda."

"I just didn't know if you could love a woman. I mean, I thought I saw signs that you were attracted to me but then it seemed like you were just being nice, so I agonized a little over that."

Kaylen laughed. "You should have seen what I went through. When I realized how much I wanted to be with you, I almost lost my mind. I had this horror of being gay." She smiled wryly. "Shows you how stupid I am."

Eda laughed her tinkling melody. "So, are you gay now?"

"I guess, aren't I? Aren't you?"

Eda shrugged. "I've never really put a label on myself."

"Well, which do you like best, women or men?"

"Women, I guess, although I've only been with women before. So it's kind of hard to be sure. I like the way women look, and their company. I've never been attracted that way to any man."

Kaylen was amazed. "You mean you've never done this with men before?"

"Made love? No. What's wrong with that?"

"But you said you were twenty-five."

"I am."

"How could someone be twenty-five in today's society and still be a...a virgin?" She choked a little on the last word.

"I just never took the time, Kaylen. I was pawed a little bit behind the bleachers during football games but was pretty much repulsed by the guys' heavy-handedness and knew I wanted something different. It got boring, what can I say? Not every teen is a walking hormone. And I had other things to do."

"God, listen to me." Kaylen crushed out her cigarette and came around to Eda's side of the table. Gently she scooted Eda's chair from beneath the table, as if Eda were weightless, and knelt in front of her, laying the side of her face against the younger woman's chest.

"I'm a stupid old woman, who is living by cliches and other people's expectations. I'm sorry. Just give me a little time to learn all these new rules."

Eda embraced her and kissed the top of her head. "Take your time, *old* woman, there are no rules really, except learning to listen to your own heart."

"I hear your heart," Kaylen said, raising her head, "and you know what it's telling me?"

Eda played along. "What?"

Kaylen pulled Eda from the chair and onto the floor of the dining room. Eagerly she pulled apart Eda's robe and began kissing her slowly from head to toe, exploring terrain that was becoming more familiar each hour. They pressed together, bodies finding new levels of pleasure.

Much later, as they lay side by side on the floor, Kaylen spoke, her voice muted and thoughtful. "I can't believe you chose me. Of all the other people you know, you chose me."

"I knew immediately it had to be you," Eda answered. "When I saw you struggling with that window, so mad and exasperated, I got this strange lurch here," she showed Kaylen by laying her hand on her lower abdomen, just above the dark gold of her pubic hair. "And my panties got wet, I swear. I'd never felt anything like it."

Kaylen nodded her understanding, remembering a similar feeling late one night watching a friend in college pushed up against a Volkswagen bus by her boyfriend, who was so frantic with desire he'd ripped her panties off and taken her, upright against the bus, right there in the 7-Eleven parking lot, not caring who saw. Kaylen had experienced a lurch of desire such as Eda described.

Eda took her hand and held it gently. "So I'm the first woman you've been with?"

"Yeah, thinking back, I desired a few, but was always too afraid. A good southern girl just doesn't do these things."

147

Eda giggled. "Bullshit. They just don't talk about it, is all. So, what was different this time? Why did you make love with me when you didn't with the others?"

"Well, timing I guess. It's because of where I am in my life and...and I'm alone and bored with my life. Here you come along all bright and happy, making me eager to get out of bed in the mornings. I guess you were just irresistible. I fell in love with you."

Silence entered the room and the women relaxed on the cool floor, lost in these new emotions.

Later, laughing, Eda pulled Kaylen up and into the shower where they playfully lathered each other, enjoying the sensuality of soap against skin and a cascade of hot water.

Ravenous with hunger, they went back to the kitchen to heat rolls from the night before, slathering them with rich butter and some sweet cherry jam put up by Eda's grandmother. Eda called Suzanne saying she was taking the day off. They spent the rest of the morning getting to know one another, sharing memories and bodies again and again. No one bothered them and they were able to pretend they were the only two lovers in a forgiving world.

CHAPTER TWENTY-EIGHT

Kaylen stared at her father's partially bald, speckled head as he fretted. She noted how small he looked in his industrial-sized wheelchair. Her mind was far away, still wrapped up in the languor of Eda's body beneath the warm, disheveled sheets that morning. The soft goodbye kiss they'd shared lingered in her memory and she wanted to return there, to feel Eda's hands on her body.

"They treat me like I was nothin' now you don't come take care a me," Joseph complained petulantly. "I don' know where you been but you done forgot about yore Pa that's for sure."

Kaylen, as she had promised the week before, was sitting primly in the orange vinyl chair next to the window. She was dressed in a floral polyester/cotton blend dress and looked the part of the dutiful southern daughter. But no matter how hard she tried for a look of daughterly concern, a contented smile just wouldn't leave her features.

Joseph noticed her enigmatic humor. "I don' know what gets in you, Kaylen girl. It's a good thing yore poor ol' ma died when she did. It just wouldn' a done for her to see how you turned out. I guess she'd be right here alongside me in this hell of a place if she'd a lived." He brushed at an imaginary tear with one gnarled, arthritic hand.

The fact he used her cherished memory of her mother against her was typical of his special form of abuse but for the first time in her life, her back didn't tense and anger didn't flare. She realized she could finally be in the same room with him, hearing his voice, and not have fragmented flashbacks of his hands on her body or his raging genitalia inches from her face.

Was her relationship with Eda helping to heal her at last? Or had the healing begun earlier, when she realized how her possibilities for happiness had been stolen from her at such an early age?

"Well, say somethin', you little shit," Joseph snarled, eyeing her with an old man's bitter anger.

Sudden compassion for her father welled in Kaylen as she thought of his life. How hopeless he must have felt as a child, raised dirt poor by ignorant, abusive parents. She felt he did love her, in his own way, and had shown her in the only way he knew how. He didn't know how to show love properly. He'd never learned because there had been no one to teach him.

Perhaps if her mother had lived, she would have eventually tempered Joseph. After all, why had a woman, a woman with money and position, who could have had any man she wanted, chosen Joseph? He'd been handsome, true, with dark hair and vibrant blue eyes, but there had to have been something more, some spark of something in Joseph Beale.

Kaylen watched him closely, looking for a sign of what had attracted her mother, as he fumed and fretted. Absently, her hand came up to fondle the heavy necklace Eda had given her. The scent of the fragrant oils with which it had been anointed wafted up to please her nostrils.

"Daddy, calm yourself now. You're gonna bust a blood vessel if you keep this up," she said softly.

"Yeah, like you'd care. You go on out there and live it up while I sit in this place and rot." He worked his mostly empty gums with angry haste.

"Now just what would you be doing if you weren't here, Daddy? You can't take care of yourself anymore and here you have heat in the winter, air conditioning in the summer, television anytime you want it, and people to make sure you don't screw up your medicine. I think that's a fair arrangement."

He glared at her, his eyes stolen from a horror movie. "You would think that."

His tone changed, became wheedling. "Why'nt you take me home with you? Just for a few days? Be just like ol' times, wouldn't it, baby gurl?"

Saliva glinted on his shiny lower lip and Kaylen felt a sudden coldness invade her, nausea welling until she felt she must surely faint or die. Instantly, she was once again transported back thirty years. Why did he continue to affect her this way?

Hastily, she rose to her feet, her ring of keys falling from her lap to the cracked, yellowed floor with a solid jangle. The sound both terrified her and brought her back to the present.

"Daddy, I gotta go," she said, deliberately calming her fear.

"And just where are you off to in such a hurry?" he asked, panic sneaking into his face.

"I— errands, stuff like that," she said absently as she retrieved her keys from the floor. His sadness touched her. "Is there anything you need, Daddy? What can I bring you next week?"

"Next week? You ain't comin' afore next week?"

Kaylen shrugged. "I don't think they like us coming here too much, Daddy. It kind of messes up their routine."

His eyes snared her again and she was surprised at his lucidity. "Hell if that's so. You just don' wanna come see me, is all."

Kaylen nodded pensively. "That is true, Daddy, I won't lie to you. You have done unspeakable things to me in my life. Things

151

that should not have been done to an adult, you did to an innocent, trusting child. I have to deal with that now and sometimes it's not too damned easy."

Her voice was calm but her mouth twitched nervously. Joseph was quiet for some time, as if chewing on what she'd said. His right hand idly scratched at his upper thigh.

"I wouldn't have touched you if you hadn' wanted it so bad," he said finally, his tone imperious.

Kaylen's chin dropped. "Wanted it? What the hell are you talking about?" Her heart raced in her chest with fearful thuds. Guilt swamped her, bitter with age and hiding. What would he say next?

"Shoot, you loved every thin' I did to you, wanted it bad. I knew that when I saw you in the tool shed with that neighbor boy, what was his name?"

"Kim Ashley," Kaylen whispered dejectedly. "She was a girl, Daddy."

"Hmm? Oh, that's right," he continued without really hearing her.

"That Ashley boy. Had his finger up you good, he did, and you just moanin' and wigglin' to beat the band." He cackled gleefully. "Thought I'd better get on that thing afore all the other boys did."

Horror goose-stepped along Kaylen's spine. She remembered the time with Kim. Kaylen had wanted it, in a sense, with the rampant curiosity of a six-year-old. And it had felt good, she remembered that, because she trusted Kim. She was so gentle with her.

She saw again her friendly, merry eyes as she teased her. Kim had been ten years old then, but seemed so mature, so poised. There wasn't anything she didn't know and Kaylen had been fascinated by this knowledge and by Kim's sense of fun and adventure.

It was this subtle memory of Kim that had unconsciously sustained her for the past thirty-five years — the memory of the heated skin under her fingers, the toast smell of flesh. And best of all, the love Kim harbored for her—a love she had had to fight to subconsciously remember and believe all these years.

Their innocent sexuality had grown naturally. Their loving had been so naive. Kim had held her, caressing and providing all the physical and emotional love the death of her mother had left unfulfilled. She seemed to want nothing from Kaylen other than her closeness and warmth.

A scene flashed before her eyes as the room with her father in his wheelchair faded. She saw Kim's father backhanding his child in the small diner that burned down more than twenty years ago, laying open the tender flesh of her full lips. The baby Kaylen had kissed those lips later, in the safe harbor of their tool shed.

She saw Kim smiling bravely at her as they wept over arms covered with stab wounds from an ice pick, cigarette burns making Kim's back so sore, she couldn't lie down. And Kim always seemed to be the one comforting Kaylen, comforting her when it was she who needed to be comforted.

The day Joseph had been remembering was during an especially bad time with Kim's father. The drinking at Kim's home had escalated, her mother drunk and oblivious to the new tortures enacted by her husband onto their daughter. New strap marks crisscrossed Kim's back and the corners of her neat mouth had been split by violence.

For the first time, her eyes had been scared and she and Kaylen had clung together, Kaylen's baby hands soothing Kim's lean, hollowed cheeks. Kim had caressed Kaylen's tiny form with frantic haste, seeking heat and solace. As she caressed her, clothing had loosened and skin had contacted skin, the feeling delicious to both of them. Kim's warm, bloody lips had rested against Kaylen's neck as she sat in Kim's lap, their breath hot and substantial.

Standing in the Appledale Nursing Home, Kaylen vividly remembered pulling Kim's hands between her legs, pulling her as close as she could, trying to ease the pain. She had been crying.

When Joseph had burst in on them, forever shattering their sacred haven, they had scattered in fear, never to meet again.

Two weeks later Kim was dead, her neck broken. People said she had tied a rope around her neck, tied it to the rafters, then leapt from the loft in her parents' barn. And Kaylen was left alone. With Joseph.

Kaylen wasn't breathing.

Luckily, a nurse's aide entered then, holding a tray. The aide, Cora Hughes, lost her cheery smile as soon as she entered the room and saw Kaylen's condition.

"Oh, Lord," she cried, dropping the tray with a sploosh of gelatin and mixed fruit. She rushed to Kaylen's side and grasping her by the shoulders, gave her a determined shake. Kaylen's head lolled drunkenly for a moment as the aide shook her and her lungs filled with a mighty hurricane of indrawn air.

"Are you all right, ma'am?" Cora asked, her words slow and precise.

Kaylen came back to the present with a harsh jolt. How had she managed to lock Kim away so effectively? How many more things had she suppressed and lost? Kim's death consumed her and she felt grief take over. Tears welled and overflowed along her quivering cheeks.

"Oh, honey," Cora said soothingly. "What is it? Are you in pain?"

Kaylen nodded, tears continuing to fall unchecked.

"Here, sit down then, let me fetch a doctor. I won't be but a minute."

Pressing Kaylen into the orange chair, she fled the room, the crepe soles of her nursing shoes squishing loudly.

Kaylen raised her eyes to look at Joseph and he actually seemed shocked by the pain emanating from his daughter.

"Kaylen, gal, you gonna be all right?" he asked timidly, stepping gingerly on ground he hadn't trod before.

"I don't know whether to kill you for the asshole you are, or thank you for giving me my memory," she said softly, rising.

Moving slowly as if underwater, she crossed and softly kissed his balding head in an absent, automatic gesture.

"I'll see you next week, Daddy. Tell them to call if you need anything and I'll bring it."

And she was gone, long before the worried aide could rush in with the fat, white-coated house physician in tow.

CHAPTER TWENTY-NINE

Kaylen needed someone. She wanted to talk about what she had remembered, wanted to rage in anger and pain and have someone understand. Eda was not at Kaylen's house; there was no green truck outside the closed, locked house. She turned her car around and headed back toward town.

Freshwater was moving slowly this early on a Tuesday morning. The only places doing any business were the breakfast diner on the corner of Second Street and Catholic Boulevard, and the gas station south of town.

Her hands still shaking, Kaylen almost turned onto the road where Suzanne's greenhouses were but remembered that Eda had gone to Raleigh to pick up trees for a second job she had begun.

Dispirited, she pulled over, preparing to return home. Spying the dismal brick library, she had a sudden desperate desire to see Jane Anne and remembered that she worked afternoons this week. She would be home.

Jane Anne lived in a small cottage that had once been the gatekeeper's home for the North Acres estate, an estate which now belonged to the Wallace family, big money that had recently arrived from Connecticut.

The Wallaces had taken the abandoned Jackson house, which had once been a beautiful mansion, and returned it to its former glory as well as adding three new wings and impeccably landscaped formal gardens.

Now as Kaylen turned into the grounds through wide brick arches, she didn't savor the view as she normally did, only stared unseeingly at the sweeping drive lined with huge pine trees.

Jane Anne's house and drive was on the left as soon as one entered the grounds. Her kitchen light was on and her car, an older model Bronco, rested in the parking space Jane Anne had outlined in railroad ties. Breathing a sigh of relief, Kaylen parked behind Jane Anne's vehicle and walked along the crumbling brick walkway.

Jane Anne had been writing, working on her novel. Kaylen could tell because her computer screen glowed green behind her as she opened the door. She was surprised to see Kaylen but a wide, welcoming smile lit her face as she ushered her in.

"Hello, sweetie, what brings you out this early? I thought you gardened until noon every day." Her voice was full of amusement and friendly mischief.

Jane Anne was a welcome sight to Kaylen. She was so dependable and normal after the revelations of the morning. Dressed in baggy sweatpants and a Myrtle Beach T-shirt, longish, graying hair loose and swept to one side, she regarded Kaylen curiously with calm, dusky blue eyes.

"I was visiting my father and thought I'd stop by and see you," Kaylen said in a subdued tone.

Jane Anne closed the door behind her friend and pressed her lips together in a thin line. "Was it very bad? I know how you hate to go see him."

Kaylen sighed gratefully, glad to be with someone who cared. Suddenly, she felt better, no longer harried and compelled to spew her pain.

"Can I stay awhile? I don't want to be alone."

Jane Anne smiled and led her into the small family room. "You have to ask? Sit down, I'll get tea. Have you had breakfast?"

"Yes, I'm fine," she said.

Jane Anne returned from the kitchen and sat on the sofa next to Kaylen.

Kaylen was fidgeting with the edge of a library arts magazine on the end table but she finally abandoned the gesture and turned to face her friend. "I remembered today that I loved someone once," she revealed in a whisper.

"Only one person?" Jane Anne's voice was subdued as well.

Intimacy swelled and surrounded the two of them and Kaylen felt grateful for the security.

"Most people love many times in their life, Kaylen, honey," Jane Anne continued.

"I know," Kaylen replied with a shrug, eyes cast down into her lap. "I'm just finding that out."

Silence stretched.

"I just never loved anyone, remember? We've talked about this. But today I remembered someone, a little girl, a friend, ten years old. I really loved her."

"What happened?" Jane Anne reached out and laid one palm on top of Kaylen's folded hands. The touch seemed electric and she quickly took the hand away.

Puzzled by the touch and its effect on her, Kaylen nevertheless focused her attention and continued. "She died, killed herself. Or so everyone said. I think maybe her father had something to do with it."

"Why would a daddy kill his daughter?" Jane Anne asked, her upper teeth sinking into her bottom lip.

"He did all sorts of things to her, beat her, stabbed her with an ice pick." Kaylen paused, her voice hitching in pain. "Molested her."

Jane Anne hissed in a shocked breath. "Oh, my God, how could someone do that to their child?"

Kaylen laughed, the sound out of place and weary. "See, Jane Anne, I've told you a lot of people don't live by your proper southern ways. There's a lot of sick people in the world." Her voice rang hollow as she thought of her own life.

"Even if Kim's father didn't tie the rope around her neck or throw her from the hayloft, he still killed her, in creeping, subtle ways, destroying her self-esteem, self-worth until dying seemed the only thing she could do right, just for herself," she continued.

"God, it fair makes my stomach ache, Kaylen, to think of that little girl..." She shook her head.

The shrill whistle of the teakettle sounded and Jane Anne rose to answer its call. Kaylen sat unmoving, thoughts of Kim filling her, until her friend returned with a tray bearing cups and a pot of steaming tea. Curling her fingers around her tea mug, Kaylen enjoyed the warmth, willing it to travel throughout her body. "I really, really loved her," she murmured.

"I'm so sorry that she passed," Jane Anne said. "What happened to make you remember her?"

"Something my father said."

Jane Anne waited expectantly. Finally she said, "You must have been very young yourself."

"Yes."

"Did her family live near yours?"

"Yes, the next farm over. They were Ashleys."

Jane Anne nodded as if that explained a lot.

The words erupted from Kaylen in a pained stream. "See, everyone thought she was a boy and...they...you know, treated her like that, bad. She worked so hard every day...farming. They cut her hair...her curls off, and called her names."

Silence conquered the room and weighted some of the raw grief.

"I wish I could have had your childhood," Kaylen said suddenly.

Jane Anne, still clearly troubled by her friend's pain, drew back against the sofa.

"Why?"

"Because it was so wonderful. Why do you think?"

"Hmm. It wasn't that great," Jane Anne said, sipping her tea. "My mama may have been an angel with all her society friends but when I was alone with her she was an iron-clad bitch."

"No way." Kaylen was interested, never having believed her friend's claims about her mother until this very minute.

"I always felt I was in training for the Miss America pageant. 'Don't eat that starchy trash, Jane Anne,'" she mimicked convincingly. "'It'll go straight to your thighs and then where will you be. Stand up straight! What are you wearing? I wouldn't wear that to a dogfight.'"

Kaylen laughed at Jane Anne's comical faces as she mimicked her mother.

"There that's better," Jane Anne said, smiling. "I like it when you laugh. It makes me feel a whole lot better."

"Me too," Kaylen agreed. "I always know where to go to be cheered up."

"Good. I'm glad I can be here for you."

They smiled fondly at one another. Jane Anne reached to pour more tea.

"Hey, what happened with David," Kaylen asked. "Does everyone in town know yet?"

Jane Anne sighed deeply. "Sure, how could a thing like that be kept secret?"

"Is he okay?"

"Yes and no. He and Kit are putting up a fortified front but I wonder how long it can last."

"I hope they stand their ground," Kaylen replied firmly.

"How do you feel about gay people? Doesn't the fact that he's queer bother you?" Jane Anne asked casually, as her eyes scanned Kaylen.

"I say live and let live, life's too short."

Jane Anne pondered her friend warily. "When did this attitude start?"

"Always really." Kaylen shrugged.

For one crazy moment, she had a deep desire to tell Jane Anne about her relationship with Eda, but knew it was a foolish whim. In fact, she wanted to tell the world how happy Eda made her, how her body sang when Eda smoothed her small hands across it and how their kisses made the earth spin away from beneath her feet.

"Do you think they'll have to leave town?" Jane Anne studied the henna color of her tea as if seeking the answer there in the depths.

"I don't know. Is the story true?"

"Does it matter?" Jane Anne countered.

"I guess not. Do you think Kit knew about him?"

Jane Anne thought a moment. "Yes, yes, I do. And I think she still loves him, regardless. You know, I've read about the people in California who have those 'open marriages' and all. I think maybe she doesn't care what he does recreationally, as long as he comes home."

"Seems pretty scary," Kaylen sniffed, "but I guess love and sex can be two very different things."

"Yes, I suppose so."

After a prolonged silence, talk turned to Jane Anne's novel, a torrid romance she had been working on for two years. Comfort stole over the two of them and Kaylen felt a knot deep inside come undone. The sensation was pleasant and invigorating.

CHAPTER THIRTY

"I can't believe your father had the nerve to take advantage of you that way. It's such a stupid assumption to think you want sex madly just because you cared for what he thought was a little boy," Eda said. "It's like saying because you love sex with your lover, you'll love sex with everyone else."

They were in Kaylen's bathtub, Eda behind Kaylen and Kaylen between Eda's outspread legs. Eda was soaping Kaylen's back and shoulders, her muscular hands massaging tension away. They had been talking about Kaylen's day and the traumatic events that shaped it.

"He's a real bastard anyway. Any son of a bitch who molests children ought to be hung by his testicles until they rip off," she continued angrily.

"I hated what he did to me," Kaylen said suddenly, "and I

hate myself for allowing it."

"Allowing it, hell. You'd been brainwashed. Like so many other girl children you do what you're told. It's all conditioning. Scary, isn't it?" Eda slid her wet, soapy legs sensually along Kaylen's flanks.

"Yeah," Kaylen agreed. She idly soaped Eda's knee and the part of her lower leg that protruded from the warm, sudsy bathwater. "Did anything like that ever happen to you?"

"Sure, and every other woman I know has a similar story. With me, it was my cousin Phil. It seemed he tried to get me alone and feel me up at every family reunion. He must have tried it on everyone else, too, because the older women soon began warning the younger girls."

"Did you ever try to tell him no?"

"Of course, emphatically. Didn't do a bit of good, though."

"Why won't they listen to us?" Kaylen raised up and fetched a washcloth from the front side of the tub and used it to rinse the soap from Eda's leg.

"So how do you think this whole experience changed your life?" Eda's voice was cool, thoughtful.

Kaylen shrugged as she answered. "I think it's affected every aspect of my life, everything I say, do or feel."

"That's pretty broad."

"Well, I can't love, can't trust. All my feelings just died for about thirty-five years. And I've always allowed other people to make my decisions for me. I know it all stems from his abuse." Irritation sounded in her tone. "I've only recently been able to look at all this stuff honestly and put it somewhere behind me and move on."

Eda rubbed her thumbs along the back of Kaylen's neck, soothing. "What do you think would have been different if you'd never been molested?"

"Maybe I could have loved a woman earlier or at least made Chuck respect me more."

A silence steeped in regret wrapped thick arms around them.

"Tell me what he was like," Eda requested softly.

"Big, loud. A hunter, fisherman. He couldn't understand women and so considered them, or anything they did, foolish. As long as he was well fed, his house was relatively ordered, and the sex was regular, he didn't complain or want anything more." She paused to reflect. "I'm glad he passed on, though. He never could have dealt with all the changes I've been going through lately."

"Did he know about what your father did to you?"

Kaylen laughed harshly. "Are you kidding? We never even talked about our sex life, much less about what happened before."

Eda shook her head sadly. "Stupid, stupid. It seems he would've asked. You know, just to get to know you. Don't married people know everything about one another?"

"Not in the south, baby. Ignorance is bliss," Kaylen joked. "These people believe that if you don't talk about it, it might go away," she added more seriously.

Eda laughed her wind chime laugh. "No, the people around here believe that if they talk about other people, they'll keep the gossips so busy they won't be able to talk about them and what they're doing."

"Amen," Kaylen agreed with a hollow laugh.

Eda reached around and began to lather soap across Kaylen's breasts. Kaylen sighed in pleasure and pushed Eda's hand lower, to the dark fur adorning the cleft between her legs.

"And what about us?" Kaylen asked dreamily.

"Well, we could get married, settle down and start a family." Laughter sang in Eda's voice.

"Please, Eda," Kaylen said in reprimand. "Really. What happens if people find out about us?"

Eda sighed. "They find out. I'm not ashamed of loving you."

"I'm not either, but we'd probably have to leave town like poor David."

"If David leaves town because people are talking about him, then I think he's the one with the problem. No matter who we love or what we do, short of murder or maiming, we still have the right to live in Freshwater. I mean, we're not hurting anyone, are we?"

"It doesn't matter," Kaylen warned. "We'd be oddities, outcasts."

Eda still sounded unconcerned. "I don't know about you, but I've always been a little odd and since I don't socialize much, I guess I already am an outcast of sorts. How could it get worse?"

"I love you," Kaylen said softly, one hand reaching to caress Eda's forearm. She turned her head and laid soft lips against the inner flesh of her lover's arm.

"And I love you," Eda replied. "I respect you too, a lot. In fact you amaze me."

Kaylen turned to look at Eda. "Me? Amaze you? How?"

She paused and took a deep breath. "Well. You're like some rare, beautiful bird that I've been fortunate enough to stumble upon, a *rara avis* which has miraculously entered my life. I'm so glad I found you." Eda's arms tightened about Kaylen, turning her so their lips could meet.

"I've never been this happy," Kaylen murmured against Eda's neck.

Eda chuckled. "Come into the bedroom. Maybe we can make you even happier."

CHAPTER THIRTY-ONE

Eda spent the night at Kaylen's house and they rose early, breakfasted, then immediately began work on the yard. The small crew that had helped shape the project was gone, paid off the week before. The only remaining work was the planting of bulbs and a regular mowing; jobs Eda felt she and Kaylen could handle easily.

They worked hard all morning, Eda mowing the wide expanse of grass and clipping the weeds along the walkway, and Kaylen planting box after box of bulbs in the circular gardens on either side of the front yard and the house.

The day was a scorcher with a hot wind blowing from the southwest and temperatures hovering right below one hundred degrees. Kaylen left her work often to fetch pitcher after pitcher of iced water from inside. A storm threatened about eleven but it passed over, leaving only a few fat drops to sizzle on the sidewalk. They stopped for a lunch of cool gazpacho and bread, talking amiably about a new county ordinance that would affect Eda's parents, forcing them to move a long line of fencing, a major undertaking.

Eda told Kaylen she wanted her to meet her parents.

"What are you going to tell them about me," Kaylen asked with a snort of laughter. "That I've adopted you?"

Anger invaded Eda's voice. "No, I've told them you're my friend. And you are, aren't you?"

"Yes, but really, I'm forty, too old to meet your parents. I don't think it's a good idea."

"Come on, Kaylen, please?" Eda used her best wide-eyed puppy-dog look to snare Kaylen's affections. It worked.

"All right," Kaylen conceded, "I'll meet your parents, you set it up."

"We can go there any Sunday for dinner. I've already asked," Eda replied gleefully.

Back outside, they leapt with enthusiasm into the last leg of their yard work. Kaylen soon realized she was pausing often to stand back and survey her new, lovely yard.

True to Eda's plans, waxy, green azaleas now rested against the white siding of her house, planted in two long gardens that stretched horizontally across the front. The azalea gardens had shorter greenery planted in the foreground and were bordered by long four-inch by four-inch lengths of weather-treated wood.

Two mock orange bushes, one on either side of the concrete steps leading to the wide veranda, were already beginning to burst into fragrant bloom. New fruit trees, a Yellow Delicious apple, a freestone Elberta peach, and even a Nanking cherry tree, bloomed haphazardly in her side yard. The occasional flower had already blossomed under the trees in neat little beds full of greenery. New graveled and bordered walkways branched off the front walk just before the porch steps and led to the vegetable garden in back. Short, woody foliage, dusky green but bearing the muted purple color of lavender stalks, outlined the curving paths. The scent was captivating, new soil, new plants, and Kaylen even fancied the air was richer with oxygen than it had been before. She reached out and grasped the willow tree standing in the garden she had been planting, whiplike branches swaying in response to her gesture. How nice it all was!

"It's amazing what money can buy," Kaylen murmured quietly.

"What'd you say?" Eda asked. She was on her hands and knees, clipping weeds along the edge of the front walk.

"I said, it's amazing what money can buy."

Eda sat back on her haunches and peered up at Kaylen. "Do you like what we've done? Is it what you wanted?"

"Yes, absolutely. I'm very pleased."

Eda grinned at the lopsided praise and bent back to her task. "Yeah, and a lot more would get done if some of us would quit admiring it and get back to work," she said teasingly.

Kaylen groaned, but dutifully returned to her own work. She had planted only a few bulbs when Eda's voice snared her.

"What are you doing?" Eda asked, her tone quick and sharp.

"Planting bulbs, what's the matter?"

"Oh, no." Eda lifted an empty box. "Where did you plant these?"

"In this circular row you laid out. Just like you told me."

"And these?" She held a second, smaller box. "Where are these?"

"Outside the others. What is wrong with you?" She frowned as she tried to figure out what had Eda so concerned.

"Oh, no. Kaylen. I told you to plant this box here, and this box in the outside circle. Now you've gone and screwed up the whole design."

"I did not!" Kaylen protested hotly. "You told me to put these here and these over here."

"I'm not that stupid. Now the shorter tulips will come out behind the taller daffodils."

"Oh, and you're implying I am that stupid?"

"Hey, you said it, not me."

"Look, I was only following your orders. I always follow your orders."

"Oh, you're saying I'm bossy, now."

"Hey, you said it, not me."

A long silence grew between them. Then a smile crept in and touched the corners of Eda's mouth. She stuck out her tongue at an amazed Kaylen.

"Na, na na, na na, na," she said in a schoolyard chant, jumping to her feet and turning to shake her small, dirt-stained bottom at Kaylen.

"Eda? What...?"

Eda was still hopping around like a demented elf, landing on one foot, then the other. "Kaylen did a boo-boo, now she's gotta dig it...all up...and do it again," she sang out loudly.

Kaylen laughed as she watched Eda's antics. "Like hell I will. I'm not doing all that work again."

Eda stood still, breathing heavily. "Yes, you will," she said in a light sing-song, "or I'll get your hiney."

"You'll get my..." Kaylen didn't say any more because she realized Eda was preparing to give chase.

"Uh-oh," she managed to mutter before racing madly toward the front door. Eda was fast on her heels calling *Here hiney! Here hiney.*

They hit the door together but Kaylen squeezed through first and flew toward the back of the house. With a wicked, reverberating laugh, Eda locked the front door and resumed stalking her prey.

"Here hiney," she called as she advanced toward the kitchen. "I'm gonna get you now."

A giggle betrayed Kaylen's hiding place behind the kitchen door but as Eda whirled, Kaylen raced away from her into the bedroom. Eda crept slowly toward the bedroom, occasionally whistling softly. Although the bedroom was empty, Eda snickered and crossed rapidly to whip open the closet door. Kaylen was cowering inside.

"There you are, hiney," cooed Eda.

"Oh, no," cried Kaylen in mock horror, "not my hiney!"

"Oh, yes," Eda said her voice deepening and slowing as she jerked Kaylen's slimness close to her own. "It's my hiney, now."

Her hands slid along Kaylen's body until she came to the desired body part which she grasped roughly. "My hiney," she muttered against Kaylen's lips and Kaylen felt a strong lick of pure desire wash across her. Eagerly she sought Eda's lips and tongue, her hands tangling themselves in Eda's platinum, sweat-dampened hair. Clothes magically came unfastened then and they fell back across the bed, Kaylen's mouth traveling along Eda's soft, firm shoulder.

CHAPTER THIRTY-TWO

Outside, a perplexed Jane Anne stood on the front porch. Looking back at the yard, she double-checked. Yes, tools were still scattered about the grass and two vehicles were parked in the driveway; Kaylen's ragged Subaru and a small, green pickup with Helios Landscaping on the side panel.

She knocked once more, then left the porch to walk around to the back. Gingerly, she stepped onto the new gravel walkway, admiring the changes to Kaylen's yard. Just as she was passing the half-open bedroom window, she thought she discerned voices. She paused and looked around. She heard it again, and this time heard a strange, strangled sound emanating from the window.

Nervously, she approached and, standing on tiptoe, got a glimpse of the entire room. What she saw made her fall on her heels so hard her teeth clicked together painfully.

Warily, disbelieving, she raised onto her toes again and peered through the opening in the sheer curtains, something a proper southern girl would never have done in a million years. The scene was still the same, although now the bodies had moved even closer together.

Her dearest love, her friend Kaylen, was naked with another woman on top of the rust-colored bedspread, her slim body flushed and rosy, a smile of satiated contentment on her lips. The other woman, smaller and more solidly built, was also naked, with a mass of long blond hair that cascaded along her back as Kaylen unbound it. Kaylen then bent to lay a kiss reverently on the slope of the woman's pert, uplifted breast.

Jane Anne could watch no more. Tears rose and blurred her vision. Panting with pain, she leaned against the clapboard wall beneath the window. Unable to compose her feelings, she fled to her car. With shaking hands she drove slowly toward town along Route 24.

CHAPTER THIRTY-THREE

The next afternoon, Kaylen made a quick trip to Lerner's Grocery to pick up cigarettes and milk.

As she opened the creaking door and stepped inside, she immediately felt a difference in the atmosphere of the store. Thinking old Mr. Campbell, the owner, had finally begun some remodeling work, she looked around the store.

Unable to perceive any noticeable change, she shrugged and moved toward the refrigerated dairy case at the back of the store, located just past the towering stacks of dog and cat food. As soon as her back was turned, she felt an intense sense of being watched.

Whirling abruptly, she caught a furtive movement as Mrs. Canody jerked her attention back to the small television set.

Odd. Why would Mrs. Canody suddenly be watching Kaylen instead of her beloved soaps?

Shaking her head in perplexity, Kaylen moved on and fetched a half gallon of skim milk from the dairy case. Impulsively, she also hooked a pint container of vanilla yogurt, another item she felt the store stocked especially for her. At the counter, as Mrs. Canody slowly rose to total her purchases, she asked for two packs of Marlboros, the long ones. Mrs. Canody reached above her head to pull down the cigarettes, but her eyes never left Kaylen. The eyes, brown and bloodshot, gleamed avidly as they studied her.

"Are you sure that'll be enough?" Mrs. Canody asked in an exhalation of Bazooka breath, all the while propping her folded arms on the counter and shifting her large breasts so the arms would fit. She indicated the half gallon of milk with a sideways nod of her head. Kaylen was clearly amazed that the woman thought she was worthy of an impromptu question.

"Yes...yes, I think so," she stammered.

Mrs. Canody gave a knowing smirk and handed Kaylen her change.

"Well, thank you. 'Bye," Kaylen said nervously.

On her way out the door, she paused and glanced back to see the woman still watching her, lips now pressed into a disapproving line. A cold chill nibbled its way up Kaylen's spine as she stowed the brown paper bag in the front seat and crawled in after it. What did that little encounter mean? Sudden nervousness beset her.

Mrs. Canody couldn't know anything. Could she? Kaylen's mind swept back over the past few weeks. Had they been sufficiently discreet? A stark, frightening thought came forward. Suppose Eda had told? Suppose this whole thing was a joke to her, a game of "let's seduce the old lady and laugh about it later"?

Getting a grip on her thoughts, Kaylen dismissed her fears. Eda loved her, she was sure of that. Also, Eda wasn't that type of person. She felt no urge to go with the crowd, to impress her peers. Still, something was wrong. Kaylen knew this town and knew the people. For some reason, she had become the new topic of conversation. But why?

She tried to think of other things that could have caused new interest in her life. Something besides her relationship with Eda. Perhaps it was her new, harsh treatment of her father. Or the strange memory shock she had tumbled into on her last visit. She shook her head in the still, inner air of her car and pensively lit a cigarette with the glowing dashboard lighter. That had been several days ago and news usually traveled faster.

But what else could it be? The thought that somehow people had discovered she was having an affair with a woman was too horrible to contemplate so she quickly stuffed it into the back of her mind and willed it to go away.

Home beckoned like an old friend as she pulled into her driveway and she quickly carried her groceries inside. The air was stuffy but she kept the doors closed. She put the milk and yogurt away and, slipping off her shoes, settled onto the soft sofa in her living room. Though she tried to coax a peaceful calm into her mind, it remained busy, thought after thought rising like the pulse of a gasoline engine. Her heart was beating very fast as she pondered all the horrible possibilities.

Eda found her sitting there several hours later when she returned from the Clyde Jefferson house where she was installing a grove of fruit trees for the wealthy couple.

"Hey," she said as she came through the kitchen door. "I'm back."

"Hey," Kaylen said softly as Eda entered.

Eda looked at the bowed form sitting on the sofa and reached to switch on a lamp. "What's happened, baby?" Eda said gently as she lowered herself, dirty clothes and all, onto the sofa. "Are you all right?"

"They know," Kaylen whispered.

"Who knows? Knows what?" Eda asked, taking Kaylen's hand.

"I went over to Lerner's and that bitch knows something."

"That Canody woman?"

Kaylen nodded silently, averting her eyes from Eda's.

"You mean about us? She knows about you and me?"

Again Kaylen nodded

"Wait a minute." Eda rose and closed the wood-paneled kitchen door, latching the lock securely. She paused to step out of her muddy jeans and work boots, stopped by the bathroom to drop them onto the tile floor, then returned to Kaylen.

"Come here." She beckoned Kaylen into her arms and they sat cuddled face to face on the sofa, Eda's small legs wrapped around Kaylen's hips, her arms embracing Kaylen's shoulders.

"Now, tell me what the hell is going on. How could anyone know about you and me? We haven't told anyone and if we were any more discreet about it, we'd be invisible."

Kaylen shook her head, one of her hands creeping up and tugging absently at the ends of her hair.

"I know it seems impossible. I went in there and I felt her watching me. And she never watches anybody, has her nose stuck in the TV all the time. Anyway, I checked out and she asked me if I thought I had enough milk, then she looked at me this way. It gave me the creeps the way she looked at me, like I was some kind of bug she wanted to examine, or something."

Eda thought a moment. "Honey, I think you're wrong. You've gotta be. The bitch is probably in a bad mood or something. Or maybe sports was the only thing on TV today." She smiled and snuggled her face into Kaylen's neck.

Kaylen sighed deeply. "I don't know, Eda, I've got a bad feeling about this."

Eda pulled back. "Well, let's look at it from a practical standpoint. What can we do about it? Even if everyone in this whole goddamned town knows that you and I get naked together every night and twice a day, if possible, what exactly can we do to stop the talk?"

Kaylen had to smile, a little. "Nothing."

"Right. So quit worrying. People gotta talk, they can't help themselves."

"Even if they don't know now," Kaylen stated in a tiny voice, "they will soon."

"Why? Are you pregnant?" This set Eda off and her twinkling laugh brightened the room.

"Eda, stop it," Kaylen said, shaking her lover's bare leg. "I'm serious."

Eda sobered instantly. "All right. Serious. What do you mean, they'll find out soon?"

"I just know they will. Nothing can remain a secret in this place."

"I think you're wrong. If we just mind our own business and leave the town alone, it'll leave us alone."

"I bet people are already talking about your truck being parked outside so often."

"I'm working on the yard, for Christ's sake!"

Kaylen's eyes met Eda's. "No, babe, you've finished the job. And the truck is here all night, most of the time."

Eda snorted and swung her back leg over Kaylen's head so she could stand and pace. "So, is this goodbye? Are you tired of me so quickly?"

"Oh, God, no!" Kaylen rose to pull Eda close. "I can't imagine life without you."

She kissed Eda with utter longing.

"Then what do you want me to do? I won't quit seeing you. I guess we'll just have to start staying at my place."

"I've told you, I don't want your grandparents to know." She turned away and resumed chewing on the thumbnail she had been abusing all afternoon.

"Look, life is full of choices. Either my grandparents or the whole town. Besides, they're old. They don't care."

"I don't know what to do!" It was a hopeless wail.

Eda reacted quickly. She took Kaylen by the shoulders and led her into the kitchen. Snapping on the overhead light, she led her to a chair and filled the teakettle and set it to heating on the stove. She prepared two cups with tea bags and pulled soft cookies from the cookie box.

"Let's not think about it any more today. We're not even sure who knows what and we can cross that bridge when we have to, okay? Right now we know that we love each other and we enjoy being together. Let's not spoil that with a bunch of what-ifs. You with me, baby?"

"But what if..."

"No! No what-ifs!" She slammed the plate of cookies onto the table and took Kaylen's chin in her hand. With sudden anger, she pressed her lips to Kaylen's.

"You are mine, dammit! I won't give you up. Fuck the whole damned town if they can't accept that." Her gaze softened. "I love you, Kaylen, so much. Sometimes I can't believe it's true —that you could love me in return. But you do and that blows me away. I'd go through anything to preserve that and you can too. You're so strong but you won't even realize it. Look what you've gone through already—your snake of a father, the years with Chuck, the loss of your mother, of Kim, learning to love a woman. I mean, come on! Think about it. How many of these Neanderthals who populate this town could have withstood all that?"

Kaylen stroked Eda's soft cheek as Eda watched her with clear, green eyes. "How did you get to be so smart, anyway?" she asked with a tender smile.

Eda rubbed her lips against Kaylen's long fingers. "I don't know. I guess I was getting ready for you, so I could be worthy."

Kaylen laughed softly. "Silly girl."

She brushed the tips of Eda's breasts through her thin T-shirt. Eda closed her eyes and sighed. The whistle of the teakettle startled both of them and Eda jumped up with a short laugh to remove it from the burner.

"Tea, milady?" she asked, eyes twinkling as she returned with the steaming tea mugs. "Hey," she whispered with a Groucho Marx leer. "Wanna play mistress and maid?"

Kaylen grinned, her gold tooth gleaming in a random shaft of late day sunlight, and took a careful sip of her tea.

"Only if you play a couple hands of rummy first."

"You've got a deal, beautiful," Eda said as she took the cards from their wooden box and slapped them onto the tabletop. Eda dealt the cards while Kaylen sipped her tea and ate a few of the cookies. They played in silence, setting up the game.

"Eda?" Kaylen asked moments later.

"Hmmm?"

"How does...or why does your belief in the Goddess make you so secure? Nothing really bothers you."

"Sure stuff bothers me," she replied with a frown, "I hate people who do stupid, inconsiderate things. Dishonorable things."

"You know what I mean."

"Yeah. Believing in a supreme Goddess allows you to place yourself in Her hands. And, since She's a nurturer, you can trust her to do what's best for you at all times."

"But She's a destroyer, too. What'd you call Her? Kabbali?"

"Kabbali?" Eda laughed at her, "Kali, of fire and energy. See, the Goddess is a manifestation of what is in every woman. Women can be nurturers, warriors, even destroyers when the need arises. Trusting in the Goddess in all Her aspects is just another way of trusting yourself and having faith in Her, in yourself. It's all interconnected."

"You never did bring me the books you promised."

Eda laid down a trio of sixes. "I know. I've been too busy trying to get into your pants. I will, though, I promise. I think everybody should devote some energy into studying religion. A lot of people follow things blindly, saying, praise this, and praise that, when they don't even know exactly what it is they're raving about. There's a lot of ignorance and confusion out there."

"Be warned, smarty pants, I come from good Baptist stock." Kaylen laid down an ace, two, three run of hearts.

"Like I said..." teased Eda.

Kaylen leaned and smoothed her hand along Eda's ribs, gently cupping the fullness of one breast. Their eyes met and Eda's darkened with desire.

"This is what it's all about, you know? This is what makes life okay." Kaylen's voice was filled with wonder. She studied Eda thoughtfully.

"I remember sitting in church, my bottom hurting so bad

179

from my father's attack the night before, toilet paper stuffed in to catch the blood that still oozed, and the preacher goin' on about sin and final judgment when we get to heaven. I didn't want to wait. I wanted judgment then and there. I wanted God to strike Daddy dead right then. He didn't. He never did."

Eda dropped her cards and left her chair to kneel next to Kaylen, hugging her close.

"But this is right," Kaylen continued with a sigh. "This is the way it was meant to be. I'm choosing you. I want your body right now, and I know you want me. It's the way of nature, the difference in the flower opening in welcome, in warmth or closing, dying from cold."

She moved one hand down between her legs, pressing against the fabric of her sweatpants.

"I want you here," she whispered. "I can feel myself opening to you, desiring you. It's the right feeling I have always been missing. A feeling that my father's God never gave me, but your Goddess did."

Eda smiled, studying her face. "You've got it, Kaylen. It doesn't matter what God or Goddess, really. It's about what you need. A God must be like a mother, supplying and nurturing, teaching right from wrong, good from bad. If you don't get that where you are, move on until you do. It's truly following your heart. If, by some chance, 'my Goddess' stops meeting your needs, you should find something new to believe and try. You should give yourself that freedom."

Kaylen shoved Eda off her and rose to stretch. She eyed her lover invitingly. "I don't know about you, but I feel this discussion could be continued in the bedroom. It's almost seven o'clock, you know, way past my bedtime."

"Since when?"

"Since now, you bozo."

Eda grinned and rose from her sprawled position on the floor. "Okay, sex machine, I'll be right in."

Humming a tune, Kaylen strolled into the bedroom and began undressing. The humming stopped abruptly when she heard the engine of Eda's truck turn over. She listened as Eda pulled the truck around behind the house so it could no longer be seen casually from the highway and her heart chilled anew.

CHAPTER THIRTY-FOUR

Kaylen left home the next morning in good spirits, dismissing her fears from the day before as her usual tendency to make mountains out of molehills. It would be close to impossible for anyone in town to know about her Sapphic tendencies.

She was dressed conservatively, in a dress of dark green cotton with black leather skimmers on her feet. She wore no stockings however; her own small rebellion.

Today was her regularly scheduled day for art enrichment classes at Northside Elementary. She had planned an unusually creative activity for the day—free hand drawing of the planets. Her large quilted bag contained pastels, big squares of art paper, a tape player and a cassette tape of Marada's *Equinox*. She would play the music while the children closed their eyes and drew what the music inspired in them. So it was with an eager step that she approached Sid Thomas's classroom. Although Sid met her at the classroom door as usual, Kaylen could see he was subdued, his eyes avoiding her direct gaze. Yesterday's fears resurfaced abruptly.

"Good morning, Mrs. Stauder," the children called.

Was she imagining it, or were the children watching her with unusual interest?

"Good morning, boys and girls," she said, pasting a bright smile on her face. "Today we're going to do something really exciting. How many of you would like to listen to interesting music and draw pictures about how the music makes you feel?" A few hands raised but most of the faces lifted to her were puzzled.

"Good. Well, today we're going to focus on drawing planets out in space. Doesn't that sound like fun?"

The first graders continued to watch her. Silently.

She watched them back, worry gnawing at her gut. She glanced toward Sid but he was no help, reared back in his desk chair studying something outside the window. Kaylen sighed.

"Okay, then, let's get started. Allison," she said, indicating a small blond girl whom she had called on several times before. "Would you please pass out these sheets of paper so everyone has one?"

Instead of skipping forward with her usual enthusiasm, Allison hesitated. Definite alarm bells began to sound in Kaylen's head.

"Come on, sweetie," she said with a sigh. "I won't hurt you."

She held the sheaf of paper out at arm's length to facilitate the girl's approach. Allison stepped forward to take the paper, her bottom lip quivering. With rapid haste she pushed the paper aside and grabbed Kaylen about the waist, pressing her face into Kaylen's stomach.

"Please, Mrs. Stauder," she sobbed, her voice muffled. "I like you an' I wanna have you come and keep doin' the p-p-potato prints with us."

Kaylen loosened the child's grip and knelt down so their

faces were level. "Why, Allison, honey, why would you think I'd stop coming to see you? I love having art classes with you and the others."

Allison wiped her nose with the back of her hand, prompting Kaylen to fetch a tissue from the box resting on a nearby windowsill and press it to the child's face. "My m-mama says the school can't let you come no more."

"Yeah," yelled one stocky boy in the back, lisping through his missing front teeth. "It's cuz you like women better than boys. I heard my mama tell my daddy. Why don't you like us boys, Miz Stauder?" He was clearly puzzled.

Kaylen felt all the air rush from her lungs and she just knew she was going to vomit vanilla yogurt all over Allison's fine hair as well as the beige tiles on the floor.

Surprisingly, Sid came to her rescue. Rising from his desk he immediately commanded the students' attention.

"Now, boys and girls, I think it would be best if we didn't discuss things we don't understand. I'm sure the whole misunderstanding will be straightened out shortly. In the meantime, I think we should go outside and have an extra recess today instead of art class. I'm sure Mrs. Stauder would be willing to come back another day and do the music project. Wouldn't you, Mrs. Stauder?"

Kaylen managed a choked nod as she sank into one of the Lilliputian-sized chairs.

Sid lined up the children and began escorting them outside. As the line passed Kaylen, several of the tots leaned and patted her back or her knee, saying consoling words, even though she was sure they remained as confused as ever about what exactly was wrong.

As soon as they were gone, Kaylen took a deep breath and tried out her shaky legs. She could stand, but just barely. Rubbing her flushed face with hands gone suddenly limp, she staggered across the room and began gathering up the art supplies, stuffing them haphazardly into the bag.

"Man, you had it all," said Sid softly, from behind her.

Kaylen's back stiffened. Sid entered the room and closed the door.

"Who's with the children?" Kaylen choked out.

"Mrs. Shore." Silence draped between them.

"Well, what happened?" Sid said finally. "I thought you and I had a good thing going. Why did you feel the need to come out?"

Kaylen paused, an angry retort dying in her throat. "What are you talking about?"

Sid shook his head and with a deep sigh settled himself at his desk. "First David, now you. Who the hell will be next? They'll tar and feather all of us."

"You mean you're...a...homosexual?"

He eyed her with angry impatience. "Would you please be quiet!"

Kaylen studied him with new eyes. She hadn't even guessed. "But I thought..."

"It was just play, Kaylen, and I thought you knew the game. I can't believe you thought I was serious."

"No, not serious really, I thought you were joking with me, but I never thought..." A sudden insight dawned. "Hey, you were using me as some type of...cover, weren't you?"

"Of course, just as I thought you were using me. You have to do that in a small town like this or you're dead meat, as I guess you're discovering now. I just hope nobody else puts two and two together."

"But Sid, I'm not really a homo...a lesbian."

"Oh, so the rumors aren't true? Of course you are, Kaylen. I've suspected for years, ever since we had that talk about the shamans and priests that day at the memorial picnic. Remember?"

"Christ, Sid, I was half drunk that day. How could I remember anything that happened."

Sid smiled suddenly, a ray of sunshine beaming through a world of darkness. "Yeah, Marshall's apple brandy was a kicker, wasn't it?"

"But Sid, you're missing the point. I didn't even realize I had the capacity to love anyone, even someone of my own gender, until just about five weeks ago. That's when I fell in love. Before that I never even gave my sexuality much thought at all. I agonized for days over this relationship I have now."

"Yeah, with Charley Byrne's girl, we know. You mean you didn't know really?"

"No, I swear. I just never thought about it. We, we who?"

"Everyone in town, Kaylen. Why couldn't you have been more careful, taken it out of town like the rest of us do? Why'd you get so careless?"

"Careless? Christ, we've been as careful as two people could be because I've been so paranoid about this happening. Do you have any idea how everyone found out?" She watched him closely, hope lighting her dark eyes.

He merely shrugged. "Who knows? Someone just jumped to the right conclusion, probably."

"So, what do I do now?" An enervating sadness filled her.

"Well, leave town, I guess."

"But this is my home, Sid. I can't just pick up and leave."

"Stay then, but expect your life to be very different than it has been. I hope you have the strength to take it all." He dropped his head sorrowfully, "I'm not sure I would."

Silence lengthened, broken only by excited cries from the playing children outside the window.

"We can't be friends any more, can we?" Her words were locked into a slow monotone.

Sid shook his head. "I guess not. I know you're smart enough to realize it's nothing personal. I like you a lot. I've just got to protect myself."

"Yeah, I know," she reassured him.

"The big boys on the school board are meeting this evening to determine whether we should allow you to continue as a volunteer. I'm sure you can already guess what the final vote will be."

Kaylen nodded even as tears brimmed in her eyes. How she would miss the children!

An image suddenly formed itself in her mind—a tall pine tree with the word love written vertically along the trunk. As she watched, the proud, upright pyramid of the tree began to change shape. Slowly branches started to wither and fall, branches bearing labels such as friends, family, civic groups, even volunteer work.

Kaylen sighed. How much would her newfound love really cost her? And was she willing, or even able, to pay the price?

CHAPTER THIRTY-FIVE

"So, seriously, what could they do together? I mean, it all seems so...sterile, somehow."

Jane Anne studied Polly as though she were an alien creature. "Sterile? I don't understand."

It was inventory time at the library and Jane Anne was glad for the daily volunteers. It was just a shame she had to pay attention to them and respond to their incessant chatter as they worked.

Polly was counting books so didn't answer right away. "Thirty-six here," she said.

Jane Anne dutifully entered the number into the inventory form then glanced out across the library.

This time of day always brought in small groups of aimless, sociable retirees but today there weren't very many in attendance. Polly's children were scattered across the main reading room and they were being unusually quiet, most actually reading. Normally they were rambunctious when their mother was nearby. A young couple, certainly no more than sixteen or seventeen, was entwined at one of the tables, pretending to study a magazine.

"You know, like sisters. I can't imagine lesbians being... passionate," Polly continued.

Jane Anne's memory replayed what she had seen between Kaylen and Eda and she pressed her mouth into a grim line. "I'm sure I don't know, Pol. What about David and his men, do you think what they do is sterile?"

Polly's mouth flew open and she turned to stare at Jane Anne, her brown eyes growing amused. "Jane Anne!" she scolded quietly. "I can't believe you'd say such a thing and Kit just around the corner. You know she believes there's no truth to that. I told you she would defend him!"

Jane Anne sighed. "I'm sorry. I didn't mean anything by it."

Polly was counting again. "Eighty-seven on birds. A lot of duplicates too," she muttered before continuing. "Men are different anyway. They have a bigger sex drive. Though someone once told me that Byrne girl was pretty wild. I just can't imagine Kaylen being that way though. Why, I've known her and Chuck just forever."

"I never met him. Chuck." Jane Anne said quietly.

"That's right, you moved here right after he died. He was a good man. Big fisherman. Him and my Buddy used to fish Wardlaw Lake together. Kaylen would sometimes come stay with me and help with the children." Her body stiffened and she paused, book in hand. "Oh no."

"What?" Jane Anne said absently. She knelt and shifted a stack of books along a lower shelf.

"Do you think she might have had designs on me? I never thought of her being that way. If I had known, I wouldn't have been alone with her so much..." Her voice had fallen to a loud whisper and she covered her eyes.

Jane Anne stood and fixed her eyes on Polly's back as anger grew in her. Her mouth twisted into a sneer. "My God, anything could have happened," she agreed quietly.

Jane Anne calmly laid her clipboard on the rolling cart. "Listen, just keep on and I'll be right back."

She headed toward the front desk, waving to Kit and pointing to her watch to indicate she was going on break. She walked out of the building through the wide glass doors.

The day was fine and filled with the fragrance of late spring flowers. The sun was hot and Jane Anne stood against the brick wall by the entry and basked in its glow. Her mind wandered but one thought intruded above all others: how badly she wanted the sun to flare and crisp her into gray ash or, at the very least, burn away the black ache coiled inside her.

CHAPTER THIRTY-SIX

With her eyes finally opened to the social workings in the world of the secret society to which she now belonged, it saddened Kaylen that she had not been better informed a bit sooner, before she had broken the rule of not, under any circumstances, letting yourself fall under speculation. She *had* been careless without even realizing it. And now she and poor Eda were paying the price.

Kaylen studied Eda as she donned a full cotton skirt. Her small rounded breasts were bare above the waistband and Kaylen breathed a real sigh of regret as Eda pulled a sleeveless muscle shirt over her head. Eda sensed her gaze and smiled seductively.

Weeks had passed since Kaylen had visited Northside Elementary for the last time and she and Eda had become even closer—as only two people clinging together in a storm can become. And though Eda maintained her apartment on Summerhill Road, she spent every night at Kaylen's house, her truck proudly parked in the front driveway.

Kaylen had become a recluse, her old life of meetings and church socials a thing of the past. She rather enjoyed the solitude—she was able, finally, to complete several household projects that she'd put off—but perversely, she missed the gossip of the town busybodies and felt intense alienation now that she had no idea of current happenings in her town. She did know that she and Eda continued as the hot topic of conversation.

The sermon board outside the Community Baptist Church proclaimed, in bright white letters on a black background, that homosexuality was a blight on God's children. Kaylen saw it as she passed it on the way to the pharmacy. And during the first week of her sins becoming public, she had been snubbed by the finest—all the women in the Magnolia club.

"Come on, Kay, honey, you'd better get dressed. This'll be hard enough without procrastinating."

They were going to the county fair. It was a risky business, Kaylen knew, but it was also Eda's Lammas celebration. During the past week Kaylen had had lots of time to read about and study Eda's strange Pagan religion. Much older than Christianity, Eda's faith centered upon a Goddess and God and the balancing of the two gender forces in everyday life. According to the books she shared with Kaylen, the history of the faith dated back to prehistoric times when cavemen carved rotund fertility figures—fat, faceless goddesses—and carried them wherever they wandered.

She was now familiar with the ancient Pagan festivals, festivals that, since they could not be stamped out by the early Christians, had simply been adopted by them and changed to fit their gospel.

Samhain, when the veil between this world and the spirit world was stretched thin, became All Hallow's Eve, honoring the dead. Yule, the winter solstice, first celebrated as the birth of the horned God or the Father Sun, became Christmas celebrating the birth of Jesus. Imbolc, or the Feast of New Milk, became solemn Candlemas, very different from the ribald fertility festival it existed as originally. Easter, honoring Eostra, goddess of spring, became the celebration of Christ's ascension from the grave. Today was Lammas, end of July, the time of harvest, when Lugh the god of light was honored so he would return in the spring. Thanks would be given for bountiful crops and for the god's sacrifice as he descended into the underworld to fetch spring back with him.

The Christians called it a harvest festival and Freshwater celebrated with a county fair. Eda and Kaylen, tired of their enforced isolation, had decided the annual Craig County fair would be a fitting place to celebrate their own personal Lammas. Kaylen rather liked the drama of it all but was nervous about the two of them appearing together in public.

Later they would share a ceremony of thanksgiving alone, just the two of them in Kaylen's house, which had been decorated with grain and marigolds, hazelnuts and poppies. Eda had also painted a huge sun symbol, which very much resembled a lion's head, onto a canvas now hung in Kaylen's living room.

The musky scent of freshly cooked popcorn assailed them as they left their parked car in the huge grassy field next to the Good Friends Methodist Church on the outskirts of Freshwater.

A man's cheery voice blared repeatedly from strategically placed speakers to insure that no citizen would miss the first call to take a chance on the fine young turkey that had been donated for raffle by Patrick and Weezie Thomas of Thomas Farms. Each chance was only one dollar and proceeds would go to support the county fire and rescue crews.

Calliope music competed and emerged victorious as the two women paused to pay their two dollars each to enter the fairgrounds.

"I don't know if this is such a good idea," Eda said finally after the fourth angry glare they encountered from the hundreds of people swarming in the graveled lot behind the church.

Kaylen angrily stared down a few outraged glances and grabbed Eda's arm. "Why should we let them dictate what we do and where we go. Come on, baby, let mama show you a good time."

And though they rode the carousel twice, the Ferris wheel once, and screamed with fear on the ominous, shiny-black spider, it was hard to have a good time when small children were snatched from their path and adolescent boys jeered and followed them about.

"You just ain't never had a real man, is all," yelled Buddy Smoot from a weather-scarred wooden bench as they passed by. The remark won approval from a gathering of his cronies and he grinned like a small boy as he accepted their encouraging backslaps.

"Okay, I've had enough," Kaylen said with a deep sigh. "I never did like these damned things anyway. Let's go home."

Eda's attention was elsewhere, however, and Kaylen felt alarm bells jangle somewhere deep in her mind. Quick as lightning, Eda crossed the asphalt drive to the bench Buddy occupied. Several of his fair-weather friends backed up to escape the force of her approach. Buddy was cradled by the bench, however, and thus captured, took the full brunt of the small woman's anger. Shouting unintelligible sentences, Eda descended like a summer squall, her small body a blur as she kicked and punched Buddy.

Soon blood appeared—someone later said Buddy lost a capped tooth in the first strike—and Kaylen's paralysis broke.

"Oh God, Eda, what are you doing," she whispered as she rushed to grab Eda's waist and pull her away from Buddy. Eda, panting and sweat-soaked, turned her anger to Kaylen and tried to break free from the arms of the larger woman.

"You see what she done?" Buddy crowed in amazement, coming to his feet and staring wide-eyed at his blood-soaked hands. "Little bitch attacked me."

Alarmed, Kaylen saw the county cruiser of Sheriff Ronnie Sample crawl to a standstill.

"Eda, honey, let's go. That's enough now, we gotta get out of here, right now."

"Hell no, I've had just about enough of this shit," Eda said through clenched teeth as she broke out of Kaylen's grasp.

"Just because you've got all that dangly stuff hanging down between your legs, you think you're better than all us females, don't you?" she sneered at Buddy. "And the thought that a woman doesn't need that thing to get off bothers you just a little, doesn't it, asshole? Well, let me tell you something, I have never needed anything any of you idiot men have to offer. The dick itself wouldn't be so bad if we could just find a way to get rid of the brainless baggage behind it."

Buddy stood in stunned amazement for a moment but, aware that they had an audience, he made the move he obviously deemed appropriate. He grabbed Eda and slammed his pelvis into her stomach even as he tried to jam his tongue into her mouth.

Eda stiffened in shock but an instant later she held a small section of Buddy's severed tongue in her mouth and had rammed her knee with all the force she could muster into that very center of his manhood.

All hell broke loose.

Buddy flopped like a landed fish on the asphalt, clutching his groin and puking blood. The people of Freshwater, gathered for the show, converged on Eda from one side just as Sheriff Sample rushed in from the other. Kaylen was abruptly swept to the back of the crowd as she tried desperately to gain Eda's side. When the crowd finally parted enough so she could get through, she found Eda lying on the ground, detached swatches of her glorious blond hair lying forlornly on the black asphalt around her. Her right eye was blackened and her skirt torn at the seam. A trickle of blood descended from her bruised lips and one nostril.

Sheriff Sample, taking her into custody, roughly lifted her rag-doll body from the road and propelled it toward the cruiser. Kaylen followed in the melee but the car pulled off before she could get close enough. She watched Eda disappear into the heavy fair traffic.

"Imagine the nerve," a heavyset woman muttered behind her.

"Flaunting herself that way. It's bad enough what she is, to carry on and make a spectacle of herself, well..."

"Shhh! That's the other one," a second woman said, and Kaylen felt the hair at the nape of her neck begin a crazy dance. She lifted her eyes and found she was staring into the dog-lusting face of her father. But it wasn't really her father, it was just one of the dozens of old men in this town who were so much like her father. The men were watching her, rheumy eyes alight with greed and delight in her misery.

She knew in that moment that she was indeed capable of murder. Stifling her deadly intentions, she walked methodically toward the parking lot.

Later that day Eda was given a court date and released.

Kaylen took her by the clinic and had Doctor Riley take a look at her. He patched a few abrasions and declared she would recover with a few days' rest. Eda was silent, her vitality extinguished, and Kaylen felt fear swamp her. If Eda's indomitable spirit couldn't get over this, then perhaps all hope was lost.

"Eda?" Kaylen queried gently when they were in the car. "Are you okay? Please talk to me."

She glanced over to the passenger side of the car and saw that the face she loved so dearly had been subtly changed, not just battered, but also closed, locked to her in a way it never had been before.

"We can ride this through, Eda, I know we can. Just come back to me talk to me. What about all the things you've been telling me? About how these people are only hurting themselves? Remember?"

Pulling into the driveway, Kaylen walked around the car to open Eda's door.

"My mother won't even talk to me," Eda said in a hoarse whisper, her gaze fixed on the clasped hands in her lap. "Did I tell you that?"

"No, baby, I didn't know," Kaylen answered quietly as she knelt beside the Subaru.

"My brothers call and make stupid jokes. Suzanne can't

get me much work and what little she does get is farther and farther out of town." She raised tragic eyes to Kaylen. "What am I supposed to do?"

Kaylen wrapped one arm about Eda's shoulders and drew her from the car. Staggering like an old woman, Eda allowed herself to be propelled inside and tucked into bed. Kaylen stripped to her underclothing and crawled under the blankets to hold Eda close.

"It'll be all right. It will, you'll see," she chanted halfheartedly into Eda's ear.

In the days that followed, the magic began to die then and hopelessness, the enemy of spirit, crept in. Kaylen watched its approach and felt helpless as a deer caught in a hunter's sights.

CHAPTER THIRTY-SEVEN

Kaylen was dancing at the county fair. She was young again and dressed in a short leather skirt and off-the-shoulder halter top. She was a delicious sight. Men had been following her about all evening and suddenly she knew the time was right. Her feverish body told her.

Subtly she chose the first man she spied. Pompous George Adams, the administrator for Craig County. She encouraged him, boldly grabbing him at every opportunity, wiggling her unbound breasts and smoothing her hips along his groin. He responded, his puffy face reddening above his too-tight collar and tie. His short, stubby fingers reached for her in broad daylight, only realizing before the tips touched her flesh that he had a reputation to uphold.

Furtively glancing about, he pulled her away from the crowd of suitors and whisked her into the hall of mirrors which, after a brief cool darkness, turned into the inside of his office. Glancing out the window,

Kaylen spotted the courthouse square at the Craig County seat.

Frowning in puzzlement because the smell of the fair's popcorn and sawdust lingered, Kaylen nevertheless turned and smiled at the squat little man.

"How nice of you to see me, Mister Administrator, sir. There's a problem that we really need to discuss."

Kaylen watched as his lips crawled along her breastbone, his wormlike tongue, loaded with whitish cracks and canyons, sloshing at the edge of her shirt.

"Problem, yes," he muttered.

Suddenly he reared back and began unbuttoning his shirt. The bulge of his erection strained the front of his doubleknit trousers.

"I'm ready for your problem, baby, and I know I got a solution. Slip on over there and lock that door like a good girl now. Sally's gone out for an hour or so and won't nobody bother us."

Kaylen glided across the carpeting and snicked the deadbolt into place. She eyed George over her shoulder in a seductive pose and slipped off her shoes. The room began graying around the edges and she felt dizzy suddenly and feared she would be swept back to the fair before accomplishing her goal.

Rapidly she crossed to his desk. He sat behind it in his tall leather chair, his hairy chest protruding from his shirt like a baby bear trying to burrow into its mother. His penis, the bare, pink-padded foot of the bear, thrust angrily from the open slit in his trousers.

"Here you go, little gurrl, got it waitin' over here for you. Come on and make daddy feel real good."

The gray increased and Kaylen obediently moved around the desk.

The color red inched its way into her consciousness and she realized she was smeared with crimson blood. Her hands and forearms were actually dripping the hot, pungent tide. She lifted her eyes and saw her father before her, his slight form dwarfed by the tall leather chair. His bleary eyes watched her accusingly as his head lolled to one side, held to his body only by the tough stalk of backbone her knife hadn't been able to penetrate.

The knife. It was still clutched tightly in her hand. Her first impulse was to let it drop but then she remembered. And the knife descended into the hollow of her father's chest, again and again, only to creep lower until his testicles, denuded of skin, rested in her bloody hand. They looked like newborn mice, wrapped up in their little tails.

"Now that's no way for a nice l'il gurl to act," her father scolded, his voice bubbling from his cut windpipe. "But then again you always was trouble."

Eda turned in Kaylen's arms and the movement woke her from the dream. Cautiously she drew Eda closer and soothed her with gentle hands until her breathing was deep and even again. She watched as the sun's reflection brightened a tiny corner of the bedroom wall.

CHAPTER THIRTY-EIGHT

Joseph studied Kaylen calmly. "Well, surprised to see you here," he said, a smirk on his slick, blotched lips.

Kaylen stirred and looked at her father. "Yeah? Why is that? You know I try to come see you when I can, Daddy."

"But where's yore little girlfrien'? Ain't she with you today?" Glee danced in his aged, raving eyes.

Kaylen sat silent a moment, digesting this new realization. "Naw, she ain't with me today, Daddy. Some folks tried to jerk her hair out by the roots the other day so I left her in the bed. Don't worry, she'll probably come by to see you sometime. After all, she ought to have a look at the man who made her lover so neurotic."

He frowned. "Hmmph. What's this neurotic shit? What's that s'posed to mean?"

"It means you fucked me over good, old man. I never even had a chance."

"Now wait a minute, Miss High and Mighty. Don' you go blamin' me fer your bein' queer and all. I had nothin' to do with that. Hell, I don't even know what ya'll gals do to each other that could amount to anything."

Kaylen shook her head, sick at heart. "You don't get it at all, do you?" She watched him.

"Naw, naw, I don't know what you're talkin' about," he said, squirming uncomfortably in his wheelchair.

"I'm never coming to see you again," Kaylen said calmly, her eyes seeking his. "I don't care what people will say or even what people will do. I have spent my whole life doing what other people expect me to do. And I swear to you here, sir, on the grave of my dead mother, that I will never do that again. From this day on I will do what I want to do, when I want to do it and I'll do it just how it pleases me to do it. Do you understand that? I don't owe anybody anything."

"That ain't right, Kaylen. Yore my daughter and you gotta be beholden' to me for raisin' you. That's the way it's done, the childern grows up and takes care of their mama and daddies. It's just the way it is, you know that."

Kaylen rose and straightened the hem of her T-shirt. "That's for kids whose mamas and daddies loved them right, Daddy. Not for the children of people like you. And another thing."

She paused and glared at him with uncanny calm. "I'm not queer because you molested me. You molesting me actually kept me from being queer for some thirty years. Goodbye, Daddy. I'll probably break down and come to your funeral."

She leaned and touched a palm to his spotted, bald head one last time before walking out of his room and finally putting him out of her life.

CHAPTER THIRTY-NINE

"I've gotta get away." Eda stood before Kaylen, her hands nervously twisting the soft cotton fabric of her shirt into a knot.

Kaylen, sitting in the ragged rocking chair on the long front porch of her house, dropped her head with a sigh. The two of them had been drifting apart in the weeks since the county fair and Kaylen had already sensed she was losing her.

"Eda, don't leave me. I don't know if I can stand it." Her words were choked off as she pressed her face into the crook of the arm she had propped against the high back of the chair.

Eda dropped to her knees and gazed up at Kaylen. "Come with me. We can go anywhere you like. I've got all kinds of money saved up and the government can send those survivor checks you get to wherever you live."

Kaylen leaned forward and pressed a palm to each of Eda's

lean yet cherubic cheeks. "Eda, where are you going to go?"

"It doesn't matter, I said." Her pained gaze locked with Kaylen's. "Just so long as it's away from this horrible town."

"It's got to blow over soon. Then life will get back to normal."

"No." Eda pulled away and walked to the edge of the porch, her back to Kaylen.

Grasshoppers called to insect lovers in the tall, coarse grass growing against the weatherboard of Kaylen's house. The dog days of summer had descended in full bloat and hot, moist air rode the county like a blanket.

"It'll never change," Eda stated. "This town is too archaic, the people too set in their ways. I committed a crime by loving in the wrong direction and they won't let me forget that."

"So you've gotta go, gotta split us up." Kaylen's voice was bitter.

Eda turned, her face registering a mixture of surprise and eerie resignation. "I don't want to leave you here. There's no life left here for you either. You have to come with me."

Kaylen fell silent. Did she want to leave Freshwater? She'd begun life in a ramshackle house on a hundred-acre farm near the town and other than occasional visits to local relatives and her college days in nearby Winston-Salem, she had never lived anywhere else. Angry dismay washed through her. Was it fear that had kept her within the confines of Freshwater?

Thoughts whirled through her, each one competing for dominance. Her father's abuse had filtered into every other aspect of her life. Had it infiltrated here as well? Was it a lack of self-confidence and self-esteem that was holding her back from expanding her horizons? She took a deep breath and held it in for a long time.

No, she couldn't blame everything on her father. She visualized some nameless city from some television show. She saw the bustling streets, the sad, homeless people. Taxicabs passed alongside noisy, smelly buses. People hurried by with sad, stress-filled faces. Blessed anonymity was the only thing a city could give Kaylen and she was wise enough to realize this fact. But, after all, how much real anonymity could a forty-year-old woman obtain when her lover was a fresh-faced twenty-five-year-old like Eda?

"Hey." Eda stood facing her, questioning and on edge as if life itself hinged on Kaylen's next spoken word.

Kaylen planted the soles of her bare feet onto the seat of the chair. Her long arms crept around to hug her knees.

She couldn't go with Eda. She realized that now. She wasn't meant to stay with young Eda and going with her would take her life in a direction she knew wasn't right for either of them. Freshwater, even with all its bias and bigotry, was still Kaylen's home.

Her soft brown eyes lifted and she knew from Eda's face that she was able to read the answer there. With a primal cry of pain, Eda turned away and lurched down the porch steps.

Amid the heat of the day, a sudden, unexpected breeze stirred the hair at the nape of Kaylen's neck and she lifted her wet face to savor it. Smells wafted to her, familiar smells: cow dung from the grazing field, pungent grasses, the tang of a fluttering insect, the dark smell of earth and root.

Eda was gone for almost an hour. Kaylen watched her short form bobbing through the tall grasses in the hayfield across the highway as she walked out her pain. Then they were in each other's arms and the world crept silently away. Only the kiss of warm, fragrant flesh remained. And their mingling carried the poignant gasp of bittersweet farewells.

"I'll miss you," Kaylen muttered sometime later as darkness mantled the earth with a cloak of hot silk. She lay her bare leg alongside Eda's, measuring visually the differences in length and texture. Her mind snapped a photograph for later perusal, each last moment together becoming one of those truly precious moments touted in television commercials.

Eda couldn't answer. A forearm across her eyes, she lay as if afraid to trust her voice. She shook her head gently. Kaylen raised herself on one elbow, the softness of the bed drawing her closer to Eda. She looked down at the woman who had changed her life so completely, wondering desperately how to tell her what she had done for her.

Eda uncovered her face then and their eyes locked. Kaylen realized Eda already knew everything that was in her heart. The quiet, deep voice in Eda's green eyes told her that. It also told her what a special, wonderful person she was, really, no matter what her father had done. And being so wonderful, she could love and be loved.

She could also summon the courage to stay on in Freshwater, alone.

CHAPTER FORTY

Eda had gone and Kaylen was alone again, this time without even Jane Anne for company. Only this time she found she was holding more in her hands than empty wishes and idle dreams. She held herself finally, cradled just so within her own two hands.

She spent a lot of time reading, using the library in Raybun County so she didn't have to face Jane Anne and other Freshwater people who weren't quite ready to see her.

She also watched a lot of movies. The movies touched some deep creative chord in her and she began painting again, ordering supplies from catalogs. Her paintings were no longer pinched and built from specific artistic rules like the ones from her college days. These paintings were goddesses and gods, flushed with rampant sexuality. They took abstract but still recognizable forms and for a time she lived for creating these paintings, portraying color and form until late in the night and then falling into exhausted slumber.

Eda wrote often, her daughterly letters the highlight of Kaylen's days. She knew they would always be close and she read with a mixture of emotions the letter that revealed Eda had found a new woman-friend at veterinary college who was her own age and with whom she had much in common.

Kaylen's paintings began to overrun her house so she offered a few of the less erotic ones to the Raybun County Library. The Ladies of the Library in that town were delighted and hung several of them prominently.

Simona LeBrea of the Greater Carolina Arts Alliance saw them there and was struck by their grit and honesty. Thanks to her opinion, prestige and connections, soon Kaylen had her own show and, though she could hardly believe it, she became something of a celebrity in several surrounding counties.

Perhaps it was this positive notoriety, along with the passage of time that gave her the brazenness to walk with head high into the December meeting of the Freshwater Magnolias. A frigid silence fell after she entered the library conference room but Kaylen was gracious. Without hesitation, she walked straight to Polly Withers, secretary of the club, and held out a check.

"I realized the other day I hadn't paid my dues for next year so thought I'd better scoot down and pay up right away." Her gaze challenged Polly to reject her outright.

Polly glanced around the room, as if trying to gauge reaction from the other women, but in effect made up her own mind. Money was money and she was certainly willing to let bygones be bygones.

"Why, thank you, Kaylen, that was right thoughtful of you to remember us," she said, entering the amount with precise care into her receipt book.

Not wanting to press her luck, Kaylen took a seat far to one side, away from the other members. Ignoring the twittering which had begun the minute she sat down, she slipped her gloves into her handbag and laid the bag primly in her lap.

After a moment, she let her coat slide from her shoulders and tried to sit comfortably. When the group had voted on the purchase of fruit baskets for the elderly at Christmas and the collection of used eyeglasses to turn in to the county health department, Kaylen finally let her gaze slide surreptitiously around the room.

Ellie sat in the front row, Beverly in tow as usual. Jeanie was there in the second row as was Weezie Thomas and Clara Amos. The back row was occupied by Polly and Jane Anne.

Kaylen's heart leapt at the sight of Jane Anne, her old friend, and then hardened slightly as she remembered that during those awful months of persecution, her friend had not once sought her out. Nor answered her calls. When the going had gotten rough, Jane Anne had simply bailed out. But then her heart softened again.

Jane Anne looked bad, her dark brown hair streaked with new gray. She had lost weight and her nice tweed clothing hung on her too-thin form like empty feed sacks. She knew Jane Anne, how pristine and prim were her ways. It was no wonder she had avoided Kaylen. She was desperately afraid of ruining her own reputation.

Drawing her gaze away, Kaylen suddenly wanted to go home. What did she really have in common with these women anymore? She was not the Kaylen she had been. The meeting couldn't end soon enough and though a few of the women, those who didn't avoid her gaze, smiled a welcome and offered refreshments, Kaylen made her apologies and fled the tense situation.

Later, at home, she peeled off her dress and stockings, and drew on sweatpants and heavy sweatshirt as her house tended toward chill in the evenings now.

An unfinished painting waited for her, a bare female torso swathed in purple veils. Learning patience, she dallied, preparing a pot of coffee, filling her cup and sipping it as she cherished the canvas with her eyes. Placing the cup on a nearby table, she lifted her brush and scrubbed at its dryness with a soft rag. The brush sought paint, and paint sought canvas, and fantasy sought reality as the painting flourished.

Then, two hours later, a timid knock sounded at her kitchen door. Stunned by the noise, it took Kaylen a few moments to descend from her creative heaven and recognize the sound. An immediate image of Eda filled her senses and she hurried through the darkened house. At the door she paused, realizing who was on the other side of the panel. She opened the door, letting in a blast of cool air ridden by Jane Anne.

"Well, hello stranger," Kaylen said trying to make her voice light. "What brings you out after dark in this cold?"

Jane Anne fingered her coat lapel nervously, her mouth working but no sound radiating from it.

"Lordy, you must be half-froze," Kaylen said, ushering her into the living room. "It's not much warmer in here I'm afraid, I've been scrimping on the heat lately. Seems like I just don't get cold when I'm working. Beats me if I know why."

She realized she was babbling, trying to make Jane Anne feel easier, so she pressed her lips together and made a big to-do of taking Jane Anne's coat and scarf and hanging them in the closet. Finished with that, she stood for an awkward moment then headed to the kitchen. "I'll put the kettle on, you just get comfortable."

She was slumped over the stove staring at her reflection in the stovetop when Jane Anne entered the kitchen. Kaylen turned and looked at her friend, trying hard to hide the hurt she knew was in her eyes.

"I came to apologize, Kay," Jane Anne said softly, her eyes shadowed and downcast.

Kaylen stood silent, not quite sure how to respond.

"I've treated you very badly and I can't hardly stand myself." A tear pushed a path along her thin cheek and escaped onto the folded hands she held in front of her flat belly.

Kaylen felt Jane Anne's discomfort with keen intensity. Confused, she turned to the sink and began scrubbing at the small splatters of paint on her hands.

She cast about for something to ease the atmosphere. It came to her. "How about a game of rummy," she said cheerfully. "You can go first."

Drying her hands on a dishtowel, she strode over to the box under the window and took out the cold, stiff cards. It had been some time since she played.

Soon they were at opposite ends of the small table and Kaylen was dealing. The kettle sang and Kaylen poured tea while Jane Anne fetched cookies, arranging them precisely on a pink flowered plate. No word was spoken during this ritual but a sense of familiar comfort began to steal across both of them.

Untasted cookie in hand, Jane Anne drew a card and discarded a nine of clubs. Kaylen looked it over but decided against it and drew from the overturned card pile. She discarded a two of spades. Jane Anne promptly snapped it up and laid out a three two run, spades, clubs and diamonds.

"You need the two of hearts, don't you," Kaylen murmured absently.

Jane Anne discarded a ten of diamonds and Kaylen drew from the deck. She laid down the ten, jack and queen of hearts and snickered proudly. She discarded a king of diamonds.

"Why haven't you asked me why I came here to apologize?" Jane Anne asked quietly. Her dusky blue eyes regarded Kaylen.

"Do we have to talk about it?" Kaylen said with a small child's petulance.

"It won't go away just because you want it to, Kaylen, honey. I really think we have some things we need to discuss. There are some things I need to tell you."

Concerned by the tension in Jane Anne's tone, Kaylen slid her fan of cards together and placed them face down on the table.

Jane Anne leaned back but, fortifying her courage, she too laid down her cards and cleared her throat. "Well, there's no way to tell you this other than to just blurt it out and let the chips fall where they may. I just know one thing, I can't keep going on the way I have been."

"What are you talking about? Everything's okay. I know

people still hate me but I feel like you and I can get past that." Concern for Jane Anne had become paramount.

"Way past it, I hope," Jane Anne said, and then paused. "Look, I was the one who told about you and the garden girl."

Kaylen tried to let the information inside, tried to digest it, but part of her knew that if she did let this hurtful thing inside, she might never see Jane Anne again. And she had almost forgotten how easy they felt together. Until Jane Anne was there, damn it. Then to be told…

Rising from the table, she moved toward the living room. "I gotta clean my brushes. If the paint stays on, it ruins the fibers."

Jane Anne let her head fall forward and then moved toward the kitchen door to leave. She opened it, leaving her coat and scarf behind.

Then Kaylen was in front of her, brown eyes alight with fury. She pressed the door closed with a sharp crack of sound. "What the hell do you mean you told? You mean to tell me it was you who caused all that trouble? How the devil did you find out?"

Jane Anne was struggling not to cry but frantic tears brimmed in her blue eyes. "I…I saw you, the two of you, through the window."

Kaylen nodded with exaggerated movements of her head. "So, you thought what? That you were doing your Christian duty informing the townspeople about the serpent in their midst? Why, Jane Anne? Tell me what possessed you to do such a cruel thing. To destroy my relationship. Did God tell you to make me a pariah to the whole town?"

"No, no, it wasn't like that…" Jane Anne began.

"Do you know what I've been through? I have been ignored, ridiculed, spit at, hit even. And Eda, well, Eda's gone, gone!"

She raked her fingers through her hair and paced back and forth along the kitchen tiles.

She halted in front of Jane Anne. "I was able to love, Jane Anne, for the first time in my adult life. And you, because of some stupid sense of righteousness, took it all away. What gave you the right to do that? Do you really hate me so much that you would want to hurt me and deny me a chance to love?"

A sob tore loose from Jane Anne and she fell back into a kitchen chair, covering her face with her hands. "It wasn't like that, Kaylen," Jane Anne whispered, lifting her tear-stained face. "I just wanted her to go away so I could have you back."

Kaylen grasped Jane Anne's hand and caressed it roughly. "I know, I did ignore you some, but it could have gotten better if given time. You didn't have to tell."

"No, Kaylen, I wanted more than friendship. I...I loved you."

A searing pain caught Kaylen just above her stomach and her scalp prickled as thoughts fell into their proper home. Jane Anne had loved her. She looked up and saw that Jane Anne still loved her.

"I didn't know," Kaylen stammered. "I swear, I didn't know."

"Well, I tried to tell you but I was so afraid. Then when I saw you with her..."

Kaylen pulled Jane Anne to her feet and held her thin form close, soothing her.

"I'm so, so sorry," Jane Anne breathed into her ear.

Jane Anne softened in Kaylen's arms and wept quietly. Kaylen stared into space and felt electricity grow between them. "It's gonna be all right, you'll see," she murmured.

Drawing back, she used her thumbs to sweep the tears from Jane Anne's face.

"Come on, baby, it's too nice a night to waste crying. Besides, we've got a card game to finish," Kaylen whispered finally.

Jane Anne smiled tremulously. They took their seats at the table, same as before. Only this time much had changed between them and the air vibrated with a new tenderness.

Epilogue

Winter 1987

A killing frost shrouded the land in a glistening web as the winter sun stepped slowly into Freshwater. Jane Anne observed the sun's measured tread across sloping fields of white, each ponderous step of new brightness stirring misty clouds of vapor.

"Come back to bed," murmured Kaylen, her head half buried beneath a pile of blankets. "You're going to freeze out there."

Jane Anne turned away from the window and swept her hands across her shoulders, finally feeling the chill. Eagerly she dropped the robe she had wrapped about herself and slid under the blankets. Kaylen pulled her close, hands rubbing warmth into Jane Anne's bare limbs.

"You're nuts, you know that?" Kaylen told her, dark eyes

twinkling with tender amusement.

"Not anymore," Jane Anne replied tartly.

Kaylen grinned and tugged the blankets tightly around their necks. "What were you looking at anyway?"

"Just the sun. It's melting the frost."

"You looked so serious. What were you thinking about?"

"Eda."

"Eda? Why Eda, of all people?"

Jane Anne looked uncomfortable. "I...I just wish I could thank her, is all."

Kaylen raised on one elbow, letting a torrent of frigid air into their nest of warmth. "You want to thank her. I thought you hated her."

"Of course I don't hate her," Jane Anne argued with vehemence as she retucked the blankets. "I was just jealous because she had you and I wanted you."

Kaylen's laugh was low. "Quite a few long-standing feuds have sprung up for just that reason, love. How come you're her best friend all of a sudden?"

"Now, I didn't say that, Kaylen. It's just, if she hadn't come into your life we may have never gotten together, you and I."

Kaylen kissed the fingers of Jane Anne's hand. "Are we together?"

Jane Anne smiled and reached her free hand low between Kaylen's legs to cup her sex and shake it firmly in reprimand.

Kaylen gasped aloud. "Point taken. Lord, there's no controlling you now you've escaped your mama's apron strings. Letch."

She playfully rolled away, presenting Jane Anne with a view of her bare back.

Jane Anne sidled close and held her lover spoon-fashion. She began kissing all the exposed skin she could reach.

"Did you do it?" Kaylen asked quietly.

"Yes, ma'am, I did. Eleven pages."

Kaylen turned and pulled away to eye Jane Anne's face. "Eleven pages? Goodness, what did you tell her?"

"Everything," Jane Anne replied. "I told her about how horrible she makes me feel about myself and that I don't deserve it. I told her about us, leaving out specifics, of course." She laughed because Kaylen was wagging her tongue at her.

"I told her how I loved you and that if she didn't like it, she didn't have to see me again. After all, she has her own life and I have mine. And they are not the same."

"Did you say anything nice?"

"Sure. I thanked her for raising me, for all she did for me, for teaching me all she did."

"Well, that's good," Kaylen mused.

"Yeah," Jane Anne agreed. "I feel pretty good about it. I'll mail it this morning and then we'll see what she says."

"Good for you. Watch out for Mavis down at the post office, she's anti-queer this week. Most of my mail was dumped on the ground below the mailbox yesterday. In the mud."

"Whoa! What set her off?"

"I think the Methodists preached against us last Sunday."

Their eyes met and both women laughed hollowly.

"Thank goodness we've got each other," Jane Anne said.

"Yep. Now, who's going to get up and bump up the heat so we can get out of bed?"

Jane Anne smiled and eyed Kaylen with a sexy sideways glance. "Let's let the sun do the work this morning. After all, neither of us has to go anywhere."

Kaylen took the hint. "Good point. Come a little closer then."

Jane Anne complied. Happily.

Publications from Bella Books, Inc.

Women. Books. Even better together.

P.O. Box 10543 Tallahassee, FL 32302 Phone: 800-729-4992

www.bellabooks.com

TWO WEEKS IN AUGUST by Nat Burns. Her return to Chincoteague Island is a delight to Nina Christie until she gets her dose of Hazy Duncan's renown ill-humor. She's not going to let it bother her, though...
978-1-59493-173-4 $14.95

MILES TO GO by Amy Dawson Robertson. Rennie Vogel has finally earned a spot at CT3. All too soon she finds herself abandoned behind enemy lines, miles from safety and forced to do the one thing she never has before: trust another woman.
978-1-59493-174-1 $14.95

PHOTOGRAPHS OF CLAUDIA by KG MacGregor. To photographer Leo Westcott models are light and shadow realized on film. Until Claudia.
978-1-59493-168-0 $14.95

SONGS WITHOUT WORDS by Robbi McCoy. Harper Sheridan's runaway niece turns up in the one place least expected and Harper confronts the woman from the summer that has shaped her entire life since.
978-1-59493-166-6 $14.95

YOURS FOR THE ASKING by Kenna White. Lauren Roberts is tired of being the steady, reliable one. When Gaylin Hart blows into her life, she decides to act, only to find once again that her younger sister wants the same woman.
978-1-59493-163-5 $14.95

THE SCORPION by Gerri Hill. Cold cases are what make reporter Marty Edwards tick. When her latest proves to be far from cold, she still doesn't want Detective Kristen Bailey baby-sitting her, not even when she has to run for her life.
978-1-59493-162-8 $14.95

STEPPING STONE by Karin Kallmaker. Selena Ryan's heart was shredded by an actress, and she swears she will never, ever be involved with one again.
978-1-59493-160-4 $14.95

FAINT PRAISE by Ellen Hart. When a famous TV personality leaps to his death, Jane Lawless agrees to help a friend with inquiries, drawing the attention of a ruthless killer. No. 6 in this award-winning series.
978-1-59493-164-2 $14.95

A SMALL SACRIFICE by Ellen Hart. A harmless reunion of friends is anything but, and Cordelia Thorn calls friend Jane Lawless with a desperate plea for help. Lammy winner for Best Mystery. No. 5 in this award-winning series.
978-1-59493-165-9 $14.95

NO RULES OF ENGAGEMENT by Tracey Richardson. A war zone attraction is of no use to Major Logan Sharp. She can't wait for Jillian Knight to go back to the other side of the world.
978-1-59493-159-8 $14.95

TOASTED by Josie Gordon. Mayhem erupts when a culinary road show stops in tiny Middelburg, and for some reason everyone thinks Lonnie Squires ought to fix it. Follow-up to Lammy mystery winner *Whacked*.
978-1-59493-157-4 $14.95